This Kind Of Love

By

Elizabeth Castle

Chapter One

"What are you going to do?" The harsh demand was yelled with as much force as the frail man could manage.

Not what she wanted to do, Diana Kennedy mused.

"Answer me!" Lanford Kennedy continued to rage from his hospital bed.

Diana smoothed the skirt of her light blue suit and straightened her jacket before turning to her father. "Going into the lion's den."

"I already told you; we're going to fight him every step of the way."

"There's nothing left to fight for. You lost."

Lanford started to yell but instead began to cough uncontrollably. The nurse standing nearby, whom Diana was paying to watch over her father, gave him a sedative to calm him and put the oxygen mask back on his face.

Diana swallowed the lump in her throat. It was still a shock to see him in that bed, an IV in his hand, oxygen nearby, and his once virile form fading away as cancer ate at him. Six months ago he would have never allowed his iron-gray hair to grow into such disarray. He would have refused to wear the t-shirt and sweats that were now his daily uniform outside of the gym.

Thanking the woman, Diana left to grab her car keys and purse. It wouldn't be much longer.

The doctors gave her father, at most, six months to live. Diana didn't give him that long. She could see the rapid deterioration of his body despite the treatments over these past two months. His seizures were getting worse. There were days when he didn't even recognize her or know who he was. The cancer that had started in his lungs quickly spread to his brain. The metastatic brain tumors had grown quickly, and the pressure was having an impact on his cognitive functions, while the lung cancer continued to grow so much that Lanford now struggled to get oxygen. No, it would not be much longer.

Diana imagined that only the knowledge that he would no longer have control over his family and what was left of his possessions kept him alive this long. The sick feeling in her stomach because she wished he would just give up lingered inside her, eating at her like acid. How she hated the man lying in that bed.

And how she hated Raphael Rouillard for putting her in the position of having to defend and protect her family, and in turn, protect her father.

Raphael Rouillard hated her father. Years before, Lanford Kennedy had had a brief affair with Raphael's sister, Adeline, and had gotten her pregnant. When Lanford denied Adeline's claim that he was the father of the baby boy growing inside her, she tried to take her life. Thankfully she had not been successful, and Raphael had gotten Adeline the help she needed to cope with being young and pregnant. Afterward, Raphael hunted Lanford down and beat the man severely, or at least that was how Lanford told the story. It was the only time anyone had ever dared to take a hand to Lanford Kennedy. Though it had taken the court a year, and Raphael had gotten to see the birth of his nephew, he spent two and a half years in state prison after resolutely refusing to take the plea that would have resulted in a misdemeanor versus a felony, opting instead to go before a jury. The judge had given Raphael four years for assault and battery of a highly regarded member of the business community.

When Raphael had gotten out of jail early, he had vowed to destroy Lanford. Or at least, that's how Lanford told it. But Lanford had laughed, not worried about the younger man's vow of vengeance. Ten years later, Lanford wasn't laughing. Unfortunately, neither was Diana. Part of her applauded Raphael. Adeline and her son Paul were two more victims in Lanford Kennedy's long history of abuse, negligence, and disinterest. But Diana had two younger siblings to protect, as well as their mother.

Diana climbed into her silver sedan and headed toward the corporate offices of Rouillard Enterprises. She'd scheduled an appointment to see Raphael, unsure yet what strategy she might employ. She just needed three months at most. By then her father would have passed, her twin brothers, Nick and Drew, would be eighteen and graduated from high school, and she could sell her father's shares and turn the company over to whoever the board deemed worthy. She could take the money to put her brothers through college, and if she was lucky, give their mother, Larissa, the nest egg she needed to support herself until she could find a job and learn how to support herself. It was guaranteed her father would never relinquish what was left of his shares to Raphael, and if Raphael moved forward with his plans of a hostile takeover before her father passed, she wouldn't get anywhere near current value. She had no doubt Raphael would take the company apart the minute he gained control, making the shares she was to inherit worthless.

She could admit she didn't want to see the company her father had built, Cabotage Inc., destroyed. She had worked there, knew the people, and knew what sacrifices the men and women who worked in her father's factories had made over the years. The equipment they made kept various commercial fishing and shipping businesses that relied on Cabotage's equipment up and running. They looked to Lanford Kennedy and his small empire to keep their boats, cranes, and other equipment working. And for a time, those same men and women who looked to Lanford for their livelihood had looked to her for guidance and support until she hadn't been able to take her father's abuse and left.

Stepping back into the role, she found some satisfaction in taking over the company now that her father wasn't there standing over her shoulder and criticizing her every move. Since she stepped into the role, she had been manufacturing dozens of reasons why no one had seen her father lately, even to her family. She didn't want the word of his illness to spread until he was gone. And she didn't want word of her father's illness and pending bankruptcy to make its way to Raphael Rouillard's ears.

The building that Rouillard Enterprises was housed in was a modern building. The majority of the building was glass, the sun reflecting off the tinted panes. Raphael's uncle, Basile Rouillard, had designed and built the twelve-story glass structure years ago after his fledgling construction business had its first big taste of success.

Diana could feel her courage faltering as she climbed the concrete steps and entered the cool interior of the office complex. Before Lanford had gotten Adeline pregnant, Basile and Lanford had been friends. The two men had seemed inseparable for a time. They had met when Lanford had hired Rouillard Enterprises to expand his factories and his shipyard. Diana hadn't met Raphael back then; he'd been living on the other side of the country after graduating from college. Rumors were that he had no interest in working for his uncle.

Despite never being introduced, Raphael Rouillard knew who she was. On the rare occasions their paths crossed, she could feel his icy glare following her. At sixteen, she'd gone to work for her father, and at nineteen, she had stood by her father's side as the court passed judgment against Raphael. She could still hear Adeline's cries as Raphael was taken away in handcuffs.

Diana strode toward the front desk, the sound of her high heels on the marble floors echoing in the two-story entryway. "Diana Kennedy to see Mr. Raphael Rouillard."

The curvy receptionist directed her to the elevators and to the twelfth floor. Discreet lettering on the door declared she had the right office when she stepped off the elevator. Behind these glass doors, there was another receptionist. She introduced herself once again.

The receptionist, this one male, made a quick call.

"Ms. Kennedy?"

Diana turned to see a tall, slender brunette dressed in an expensive suit not unlike her own, who had been sent to meet her. "Yes."

"I'm Lydia, Mr. Rouillard's assistant. He asked me to fetch you."

Diana nodded and followed the young woman. She was led to the back of the space toward the corner of the building that faced a view of the city.

"Go on in. He's expecting you."

Surprised, Diana nodded and thanked the woman. She had been sure she'd be kept waiting. With a light rap on the door, she opened it. Raphael Rouillard glanced up at her but was talking on the phone. He pointed to the seat across from his desk. She closed the door but only came to stand beside the chair instead of sitting in it.

"I said no. You tell them to better the offer or we walk." Raphael rose to face the woman who was watching him with wary eyes.

Diana didn't doubt he knew how intimidating he could be. She wanted to shrink under his dark sapphire gaze. And she didn't like the analytical way he was looking at her. She couldn't help the impact he had on her senses every time she saw him. He had dark wavy hair he kept a little too long. His blue eyes glittered like gems, and his normally sensuous mouth was pressed into a scowl. The black and red snake tattoo that wrapped around his left wrist peeked out from under the cuff of his white dress shirt, while the dark charcoal slacks molded to his powerful thighs. This was not a man to tangle with.

Raphael continued to watch her, and Diana struggled

for a moment to remember why she was there. Nothing short of desperation would have brought her to his office. She was pleased when her voice didn't waver. "Mr. Rouillard, thank you for seeing me."

Raphael leaned over the desk, planting his palms on the gleaming wooden surface.

Diana's eyes involuntarily widened at the implied threat.

Raphael's eyes closed in on her face. "I see your father has decided to hide behind a woman instead of facing me himself. Did he think I'd show you mercy?"

Diana swallowed; she couldn't fail in her mission. The lie she'd told so many times rolled easily off her tongue. "He's out of the country."

Raphael straightened. "I've heard that rumor. The funny thing is there is no record of him leaving."

Diana was only caught off guard for a moment. "Then perhaps you didn't look hard enough. His yacht has been out of its dock for over a month."

"One of your father's many toys. But then he has so many, it's hard to keep track. So, he sends you in his place. I never took your father for a coward."

Coward? No, he was not that. But as his days drew closer to their end, she had seen fear in his eyes, something else that was out of character for the man. "I'm in charge in his absence. While he's been away, you pounced on the opportunity to attempt a takeover."

"Your father left himself wide open. His investors were easy to manipulate. Most of them haven't seen him in months. And they have no faith in you in his absence."

Diana pursed her lips. Both his investors and his creditors had been calling nonstop. She'd fielded as many calls as she could, but most were from creditors. Her father had squandered most of his money, and what money hadn't been squandered had been used to pay off his medical debts. Comfort measures at home were all the doctors could do now, and she was paying for that out of her own money. As she had told the creditors she'd spoken with, there simply wasn't anything left.

Well, that wasn't entirely true, she thought. There were her father's shares in Cabotage left, as well as some artwork she hesitated to part with. She clung to the hope those shares represented. The yacht she so brazenly mentioned had been repossessed. So had most of her father's toys, including his Porsche, his Mercedes, and his Hummer. Tomorrow she would be moving him and his nurse into her condo because the house was foreclosing, and the contents were being sold. But Raphael either didn't know or didn't care.

Diana stood as tall as she could and focused back on Raphael. "And you made sure they don't. Say what you will about Lanford, but you don't know me."

"I know enough. I saw a dutiful daughter standing by the side of her father while he argued in court that he wasn't the father of an eighteen-year-old girl's baby. I saw a woman so spoiled, so uncaring, who simply sat without saying a word during the court proceedings that decided how much, or rather how little, child support Lanford was going to have to pay to that young woman. You, his wife, your stepsister, and his sons all stood by his side. The perfect blended family."

Diana shivered at the hatred in his tone. She remembered that day well. Her father had stood there apologetically as he'd held his wife's hand. Larissa had played her part and pretended to be the supportive wife. Diana had stood on the opposite end with the rest of the family in between. Shandy, her stepsister, had been nine, her twin brothers just five. Shandy had not wanted to go, her hatred of Lanford poorly disguised. Her brothers, unsure of what was going on around them, clung to their mother during the hearing. And while the couple had stayed married, that day marked the end of their relationship. Shandy moved in with her father across the country but had kept in touch with the family over the years, everyone except Lanford, and they still all got together occasionally for holidays and birthdays. If her father knew they kept in touch, he never mentioned it.

But now he would be gone, and nothing was left of the legacy he had thought to leave.

Raphael continued. "I see a woman loyal to her father."

In a way, he was right. "I need you to stop what you're doing. Just for a little while."

Raphael held up a hand. "Don't bother. I know about your father's debts. I know about the foreclosure, and that most of what he had was repossessed by debt collectors. You don't have a leg to stand on, any more than he does. Where is he hiding? And why did he send you?"

Diana paled at his demanding tone. He knew. She had tried so hard to hide it. She should have known better. But at least she had been able to keep his illness under wraps. If he knew, he no doubt would have thrown the fact in her face. "I'm going to ask again; please wait a little while longer before you take over my father's company."

Raphael came around the desk. The back of his fingers caressed her throat. "And what exactly are you going to offer me in exchange?"

Diana stood her ground, though her heart was beating frantically in her chest. "What is it that you want?"

Raphael's fingers circled the back of her neck, and he leaned closer. "What if I said you?"

Diana pulled away and was surprised when he let her go. "Then I'd say you're no better than my father."

Raphael leaned back against his desk. "Except you're not eighteen. You're thirty-two. But you're not my type."

Diana let out a breath. "I wouldn't even pretend to know what your type might be. I need you to give me three months. After that, you can do whatever you want."

Raphael's laugh was harsh. "I can already do what I want. And we both know it. So, again, what's in it for me?"

Diana figured she didn't have much to lose and opted for the truth. "You can do it for two young men. And you can do it for their mother. You can do it for all the people who work for my father. And you can do it because it's the right thing to do."

Raphael's eyes narrowed. "I'm not completely without compassion. But your father knows what will happen to everyone who works for him, and he's not doing a thing to stop me. He deserves to lose everything he's worked for."

Diana watched as Raphael's gaze drifted away. She could imagine what he was thinking. She knew when she came it was probably futile to try to reason with him. Revenge was a powerful motivator, and he had more provocation to seek revenge than most.

Diana closed her eyes for a moment, defeat weighing down on her. "Sorry I wasted your time. And I'm sorry that you care more about revenge than you do about the innocent people you'll hurt."

Diana would have turned and walked away, but Raphael stopped her by grabbing her wrist. She glanced down and saw the head of the snake. She looked up at Raphael and trembled.

"You're right. Revenge is a powerful thing. I wonder what he was thinking when he sent you into the belly of the beast. And I can't help but wonder what it is your father thinks when he looks back on his affair with my sister."

Diana answered him honestly. "I doubt he thinks about it at all."

Raphael snarled and pulled her down into the chair. "What would you be willing to do to get the three months you seem to need for the two young men, the mother, and the people?"

Diana thought of her two young brothers, their smiling faces, and their belief that they had bright futures ahead of them. "Most anything."

Raphael dropped into the adjacent chair. "Again, what if I said I wanted you?"

Diana couldn't tell if he was serious or not. "So if I agree to some lurid affair, you'll give me the three months I'm asking for?"

Raphael tipped his head to study her. "You'd do it,

wouldn't you?"

Diana smacked him with all the strength she could muster from the chair. "You are no better than my father."

Raphael absorbed the blow. "Maybe. I learned a lot while in prison. And some of what I learned is how to protect my own. I will destroy your father, Diana. You can bet on it. But I wonder what he would think if I took his golden girl away from him, too? What would he have left to lose after that? I doubt he has much affection for his wife. I feel sorry for her and the years she has spent with such a cold man. But you, you are not an innocent victim in this. Your presence in my office is proof of that. All those years ago, you never should have stood by his side; you were old enough to know better."

"Like your sister was?" Diana tossed the barb and saw it hit its mark.

"Get out of my office, Diana. Next time I won't be so nice."

Diana rose and fled the office.

When she got to her car, she closed her eyes for a moment. She was torn between humiliation and anger. She decided on anger. She twisted the key in the ignition and headed to the office. Mock her, would he? Before going to his office, she had hoped he would simply give her the time she asked for. She supposed he was right that she had nothing to offer him. But to insinuate she'd be willing to sleep with him for that time was insulting. And it hadn't gotten past her notice that he hadn't actually propositioned her; it had been hypothetical. But regardless, her temper was riled, and she was going to start the fight she had been hoping to avoid.

She strode into the office building that held Cabotage Manufacturing. The business had been founded by her father and his older brother Thackery years ago. The company's name had come from the word cabotage, which meant the right to operate by sea, air, or any other means. They saw themselves as masters of their budding empire. But when Thackery died, leaving behind a huge insurance policy, Cabotage Manufacturing grew into the massive manufacturing and shipping business it was today.

As she strode across the now threadbare carpet of her father's failing empire, she waved at her vice president of operations, Brett Coleman.

The short, overweight man followed her into her office. He was only a couple of inches taller than she was, and his once brunette hair had thinned and grayed. But his mind was sharp, and if anyone could help her postpone Raphael's inevitable takeover, he could.

"What's up, Boss Lady?" Brett took a seat opposite Diana. He could see the flags of temper on her cheeks.

"Raphael Rouillard is what is up. He's the one behind the purchase of our stock. I've been doing some checking in with our suppliers and customers, and he's the reason we've been having issues with supplies and losing contracts. He's been putting it out there that Cabotage is on the verge of bankruptcy and that my father's absence is because the company is failing. Rumors are that Lanford has abandoned ship. I need to know what assets we have that we can liquidate. I am not going to let him take the company without a fight."

Brett smiled. "It's about time. I thought you were going to let him have it."

Diana's brows furrowed. "You knew about his plans to launch a hostile takeover?"

Brett shrugged. "I've been in this business a long time. And I've worked for Lanford Kennedy for a long time. Everyone knows he has more enemies than friends. And the scandal with Mr. Rouillard's sister may be old news, but it's still talked about from time to time. Rouillard has not been shy in his hatred of your father. I'm just surprised it took this long. But I've been hoping to hear you say you're going to fight. I have already had our financials pulled and have some recommendations on what to sell off, what to retain, and a social campaign."

"Social media, don't you mean?" Diana opened her laptop and started pulling up the reports Brett had just sent her.

"No, I mean social campaign. Your father is essentially in the wind. No one other than you knows where he is. If you don't start getting out there and letting everyone know that you're in charge and that you mean business, you'll have no way of knowing what is being said about Cabotage."

Hating that he was right, Diana pulled up her calendar. Her ever-efficient assistant had her days and nights planned. One of their biggest customers was hosting a fundraiser this weekend at his home. "I guess I'd better get my hair done and find a dress."

Brett cleared his throat. "Not to be overly personal, but sexier is better in that crowd. Everyone knows that Gilbert

Chambers can be swayed by a pretty face. And while I would never say this to one of my daughters or my wife, most men respond, whether they want to or not, to a sexy lady."

"The red dress then." Normally every feminine bone in her body would have rebelled at the thought of dressing sexy to gain business, a favor, or anything else. But Raphael was a worthy opponent, and if flashing some leg and letting a little cleavage show would get these men to listen to her, then she would.

Diana shut her laptop. "Game on."

Chapter Two

"How did it go with Diana Kennedy?" Adeline set a plate of homemade spaghetti in front of her brother.

Raphael knew she had waited until Paul was upstairs supposedly doing homework, though he could tell her mother's intuition told her he was probably playing on his phone if her exasperated gaze at the ceiling was any indication.

Raphael took a large bite. "This is amazing, as usual."

Adeline took a seat after glancing at the clock. "Kevin will be home from work soon. I'd rather he not overhear this."

Raphael set a hand over his sister's. She was even more beautiful now than she'd been at eighteen. She had his coloring and the same wavy hair. Four years ago, she'd met Kevin Matthews. It had taken Kevin two years to convince Adeline to marry him. And once she'd said yes, he'd whisked her off, after making sure Raphael approved. Raphael could tell how much Kevin adored his sister and nephew and had given his blessing. Now that their parents were gone, he, Adeline, Paul, and Uncle Basile were the only family left. And since his uncle had semi-retired, Raphael took his position as the head of the family and the business seriously. Kevin had seen and respected that.

His encounter with Diana hadn't gone quite according to plan. She had stood her ground, though she had been trembling. He had purposefully done everything he could to intimidate her. It wasn't hard, and he'd had a lot of practice over the years, using his height and looks to intimidate an enemy, or in this case, the daughter of one. At six-three, he had towered over Diana Kennedy, whom he would put at five-five, minus the heels she wore that gave her a few extra inches.

He always made it a point to know everything about his enemies, and he considered Diana one. In his office was the first time he'd gotten a close-up look at her. She was a natural blonde, had hazel eyes, and a slim but curvy figure. Her hair had been in a twist, but he knew it fell straight past the middle of her back. Just last month he'd seen her at the home of a mutual client; the dark blue dress she had worn fitted her body like a glove, and that hair had fallen in waves almost to her waist.

He wasn't sure what to make of her plea. Though he hadn't felt like sharing it with her, he hadn't vowed to destroy the company but had vowed to destroy the man. He meant what he said to her; he was not without compassion. He knew what would happen to Cabotage's employees if he destroyed the company. But he was not the young, impulsive man he'd been all those years ago when he'd first vowed revenge.

Back when Lanford had seduced his sister, Raphael had been racing cars, gambling not only with his money but with his life. After college, he'd done whatever pleased him. Racing cars gave him money he'd never had before. He hadn't been the most responsible of men. As a result, he hadn't been around when Lanford Kennedy started sniffing around his baby sister. It was something he still hadn't forgiven himself for. His parents had been decent people, but they had been older and let their children have a lot of freedom. He couldn't help but feel that had he been around, he could have prevented what happened to Adeline. And while he adored his nephew, Paul, he'd have given all he possessed at the time to have been able to stop what happened to his sister.

"Well?" Adeline fisted her hands on her hips as if she were scolding her son.

Raphael couldn't help but be amused. His sister was the one person he could not intimidate. "Well, she didn't beg and plead, as I had imagined she would. And she didn't ask me to forget my revenge."

Adeline took his wrist when he would have taken a bite. "What did she say then?"

"You always were impatient. She said she needed three months."

Adeline was confused. "Three months for what?"

"She didn't say. But she said I should do it for two young men, their mother, and the people who work for her father."

"I take it she thinks you're going to destroy the business?"

Raphael set the fork down. "I'm certainly not going to ease her mind on the subject. At least not yet. But I asked her what she was willing to do to get those three months."

Adeline looked suspicious. "Did she try to seduce you?"

Raphael laughed at his sister's angry expression. "No. I'm afraid I hinted that I'd take her as payment to wait three months. She slapped me."

"Good. You deserved it. What were you thinking, Raph? I can't say I know her, but women don't want to feel like a piece of meat or a commodity."

He didn't suppose so, at least this woman. He had known plenty over the years who would have slept with him in return for a favor. Some had, though not through coercion. "I don't know what her angle was. Lanford Kennedy is so deep in debt that he's never getting out. The two young men she mentioned must be her twin brothers."

Adeline nodded. "She thinks you're destroying their inheritance. In a way, she's right. There won't be anything left for them."

"There already isn't anything left but a few shares that will be worthless if I dismantle Cabotage. But they're young. They'll be fine. Diana, too, as far as that goes. She's not a child."

"I bet Lanford would be furious if you did have an affair with his daughter."

"I admit I had the same thought. But I have something else in mind. But don't worry about it."

Adeline handed him his fork back. "I love Paul more than anything. He favors me so much; I hardly see his father in him. Paul knows who his father is and what kind of man he is. I didn't want him growing up with some kind of hero worship or something. He even knows he has a sister and two brothers. But he's only twelve, and you and Kevin give him all the love and attention a young boy needs. I don't want this to come back on him, or for him to be caught in the middle. I wish you would stop."

They'd had this conversation before. Plans had been put in motion, ones he had no intention of stopping. Lanford Kennedy deserved to lose what he cared about most, and that was his company and reputation. But he also did not want to hurt innocent people, especially his own family. "Diana might be the key to that."

Adeline frowned at her brother. "What does that mean?"

"It means that in exchange for her three months, she fully cooperates with me. She stands by my side, not her father's."

"And how do you propose to get her cooperation? I'd say she isn't going to be inclined to cooperate after what you said to her."

Raphael thought about it. "Perhaps. But today she inadvertently provided me with her Achilles' heel."

They both heard a car door slam, and Adeline rose to greet her husband. "I hope you know what you're doing, Raph. I don't like it. And getting involved any deeper with that family is a mistake."

"I know what I'm doing." Raphael dug into his meal.

Kevin came into the kitchen and kissed his wife. He smiled at Raphael. "One of these days we're going to start charging you room and board."

Raphael took another large bite. "What can I say? I can't resist popping in for dinner."

Adeline fixed her husband a plate and then made one for herself. "Goodness knows what passes for a meal in that oversized house you live in."

Raphael shrugged. He doubted that other than a

container of milk for his coffee, there was much food in his fridge or pantry. He wasn't a disaster in the kitchen. He knew what to do when he got there. It was just that he had no interest. His sister didn't seem to mind his popping in once in a while to join them for dinner. He'd once offered to pay for his meals, and his sister had slapped the back of his head and muttered at him the rest of the night about how she could afford to feed her family. He'd not offered again.

Paul came down and joined them. "Hey, Kevin."

Kevin ruffled the boy's hair. "Finish up your homework yet?"

Paul gave his mother a knowing look. "Yes, I finished it."

Adeline smiled at her son's back as he rummaged in the cabinet for a snack despite having eaten plenty for dinner. "Good. Then you can annihilate your uncle at your game again after he finishes eating."

"Finish up, Uncle Raph. Bed is in an hour."

Raphael finished dinner and joined his nephew. He enjoyed the nights he spent with his sister and her family. He wouldn't mind finding a nice woman to settle down with and raise a family. He knew Adeline and Kevin had been discussing expanding the family. He figured in the next year or two Paul would have a brother or sister. Raphael wouldn't mind giving him a cousin. But women had been few and far between lately, and none of them were candidates for Mrs. Rouillard. And the game he was about to play with Diana Kennedy wouldn't get him any closer to finding her. But once this part of his life was behind him, he wouldn't mind dedicating himself to the project. If he didn't, his sister would start matchmaking again.

But for now, he did have Diana to contend with. He wasn't sure what he had expected when she came into his office today. She wasn't cold like he'd expected. She'd been quite passionate when she'd slapped him. And he had deserved it, no doubt. But he liked the fire he saw in her eyes. It would make his victory that much better when he had his opponent's full attention.

And she was also right. He had been discrediting her and the company. Once upon a time, Lanford's company had been a powerhouse. He had domestic and government contracts. The ship parts his company manufactured were top-of-the-line. But sometime in the last few years, business had slipped. Quality had gone down, and some of those contracts had dried up. He hadn't had to make up stories to Lanford's customers or creditors. Lanford had done the damage himself. And now when his company needed him the most, Lanford wouldn't stay and face the music. Instead, he'd turned it over to his daughter.

Raphael was not worried about her. She had been absent the past few years, and her return was seen as temporary. Raphael didn't anticipate her being able to stop him. And ultimately acquiring Cabotage was in Rouillard's best interests. Since Raphael had taken over his uncle's business, he'd expanded operations and branched out into new areas. And while construction was still the core of what Rouillard did, Cabotage would make a nice addition. He planned to buy up the rest of the available stock and absorb the business. Cabotage would no longer exist and would be another division of Rouillard. And once he was in charge, cutting corners would stop, and the business's reputation would be restored, all thanks to a Rouillard, not a Kennedy.

* * *

The next morning, across town from where Raphael lived, Diana was starting day one of her plan to thwart Raphael Rouillard, or at least delay him, by wearing her best suit and finishing the touch-ups on her makeup.

Diana applied her lipstick and left the bathroom. Her things were all over the living room. Her father was moving in this morning before she left for work, and she'd barely managed to clear out her bedroom and the spare room. Diana's condo had two bedrooms. The full-time nurse had moved into the bedroom she used to paint in, and her father, hospital bed and all, had moved into hers. Larissa and the boys had moved into an apartment not far from the boys' school so they could finish their senior year. Even if there had been room in her condo, Larissa would have opted for the apartment. And if Diana couldn't get the three months she needed, Larissa and her children would move in with Larissa's daughter Shandy, and the boys would not be able to go to the university of their choice. It wasn't the plan any of them had hoped for, but unless Diana was successful, it was the best they could hope for.

If she failed, the boys would have to go to the less expensive community college in Pittsburgh. After all they'd been through, after all they'd tolerated from their father, they deserved to go to a school better suited to their area of interest. Larissa deserved to have the small condo across town she'd been wanting. But all Diana could afford on her own was the small apartment and three plane tickets for the three of them to go to Pittsburgh come summer.

She would have to worry about all that later. After seeing her father settled, she needed to go back to the office. She had not been on her father's payroll for almost eight years and had only started going in these past three months. She still had so much to catch up on. At the factory, she'd been welcomed back by many of the men and women who had worked for the company for years, many of whom knew her when she'd been a child. Her heart ached for those hard-working men and women and the families they supported after Raphael dismantled the company. Some of them were getting to an age where finding a new job would be nearly impossible, and the thought of them losing their healthcare and benefits made the knot that had been living in her stomach these past three months that much tighter.

The only thing about this situation that hadn't been difficult was letting the bank take her father's house. Over the last few years, her father had started to spend more and more time away from home. He'd taken to sleeping on his yacht, most often with his mistress with him, and very rarely bothered to come home to the white sprawling house he had called home since she was a little girl and her mother had taken off. She was glad to see it go. Perhaps the next family who owned it would find more happiness inside those walls than she had.

Her cell phone rang, and she was grateful to be taken

away from her thoughts. She frowned and hit the ignore button when she saw the unknown number. She'd been getting vaguely threatening calls since the day she'd first called Raphael's office to make an appointment to meet with him. Leaving threatening voicemails didn't seem like his style, but then again, what did she know? He had attacked her father, after all, and had done time in prison. Who was to say he wouldn't do the same to her? But deep down, she didn't believe Raphael was behind the calls. He hadn't so much as raised his voice when she'd slapped him. But someone was behind the calls, and it was starting to scare her.

Diana grabbed her purse that she had tossed on top of her dresser, which now graced her living room. She shouted to the nurse, "I'm off to work."

The young nurse named Jasmine came out of the bedroom where she'd been finishing setting up the room for her father. "Your father is having a hard morning. The move took a toll on him."

Diana once again felt guilt gnawing at her. "There was nothing else to be done. I couldn't afford to keep the house out of foreclosure long enough for him to spend his last days there. It was either move him here or to a nursing home. I'll be back tonight."

Grateful to escape her condo, the place she wasn't sure would ever feel like home again, she drove to the office. She greeted the faces she knew by name and simply waved at the rest. Not for the first time, she noticed the atmosphere in the office had changed dramatically in her father's absence. People were happier, and the mood was lighter. Little did they know an ax was hanging over their heads. Part of her wanted to tell all of them to start looking for a new job. But the hopeful part of her dreamed she'd be able to save the company, at least long enough for someone else to come on board. Someone other than Raphael Rouillard.

Brett poked his head into her office. "Have you seen the numbers today?"

Diana waved him in. "If you mean the stock numbers, yes, I did."

"Rouillard has been busy since you met with him yesterday."

Diana shook her head. "We can't worry about the stock numbers right now. Did the shipments get out?"

Brett nodded and handed her his report. "Shipped sales are up. The men outdid themselves. That contract was an important one, and they came through."

Diana could smile at that. "I expected nothing less. Go ahead and share the report out. And I need you out at the warehouse. We've got inspections coming up, and I want us to pass with flying colors."

Brett saluted her. "You got it, Boss. I don't suppose your father said when he's coming back? This contract will have gone a long way toward making our clients feel better that we can deliver, but they want his reassurance. And we need him if we're going to fight Rouillard."

Diana shook her head. "He's adamant, Brett. I wish I could make him return, but all I can do is hold down the fort in his absence. You and I are going to have to hold Rouillard off."

Brett sighed. "All right. I'm still working on seeing

what else we can liquidate. I'll let you schmooze clients while I do that. Ready for the party tomorrow?"

Diana nodded. Her dress was pressed and ready to go. She only hoped her acting skills didn't suddenly fail her. She was going to need them to convince her father's clients to trust her in his absence and to assure them that everything was under control at Cabotage.

But by the time the workday ended, she knew it was going to take a miracle to keep Raphael from taking control. He'd made his first set of official moves. He'd filed papers with the SEC to start the process of buying up more shares of Cabotage and making his intentions clear. Then as if that hadn't been enough, she learned her father's biggest client's contract was up for renewal. The legal team had yet to secure his name on a new contract. She frowned at the name. Gilbert Chambers. The man whose fundraiser she was attending tomorrow.

Brett poked his head in. "I'm guessing you heard the news. The office was buzzing the second I walked through the door."

Diana knew it would have been too much to hope that the takeover could be kept secret a little longer. But as soon as she'd gotten the call, she'd turned on the financial news. The filing was public knowledge now. "Yes. I know."

Brett's eyes were troubled. "Are you going to address the team?"

Diana stood, straightening the ivory skirt of her suit. "Get the department leaders in a conference room. We need a plan."

But two hours later, she had no more of a plan than she

had before. The various department heads were furious and demanded Lanford return. Her firm "he's not coming back" had echoed off the gray walls of the conference room. The silence that descended had been deafening. Conversation had been stilted after that; no one in the room believed they could fight the takeover without Lanford at the helm.

After the meeting ended, Diana packed her briefcase with everything she needed to study Mr. Chambers' contract before the fundraiser the next day. As she left the office, she could feel the accusing eyes of the staff on her back as she left.

She was almost at her car when a voice stopped her.

"Good evening, Miss Kennedy."

Diana's grip tightened on her keys at the unfamiliar voice. A large, dark-haired man stepped out of the shadows behind where her car was parked in the parking garage. He was only partially in the shadows, so she got a good look at him. His khakis were worn, and the dress shirt was half unbuttoned and wrinkled, and he wore no tie. Nervous at the way he was looking at her, she glanced around, but she was alone. She was poised to run but waited to see what the man would say. "Who are you?"

"A messenger for an interested party. Where's your father?"

Diana looked around again, willing someone to show up. She took a step backward, knowing she probably didn't have much of a chance of outrunning the large man in her heels. "He's out of the country."

The man took a step forward, his tone harder than before. "Which country, Miss Kennedy?"

She took a few more steps backward, frightened as he came toward her, and fully left the shadows. "I don't know. I just know he left. Maybe try his friends."

The man showed his teeth. "We are his friends, Miss Kennedy."

Nothing in the man's words was threatening, but his tone was. Not willing to wait a moment longer, not after the threatening calls she'd received, she spun on her heels and dashed for the closest opening. The man didn't shout or make another sound, but she knew without looking he was coming after her. She was almost to the opening when she unwillingly turned her head to see if the man was still there. She saw him frown and then take off in the other direction just as she slammed into what at first she thought was a wall.

Hard arms came around her to keep her from falling. It wasn't a wall she hit, but a large chest. Diana looked up. Raphael's grim face was looking down at her. Almost hysterical, she heard the words pop out of her mouth. "It would be you."

Chapter Three

Raphael held Diana to him as he looked around. He thought he'd seen a man headed toward Diana, but he hadn't gotten a good look. All he'd gotten was an impression of height and build. The man was probably around his size in height, though heavier in the midsection.

He looked down at the woman watching him, her eyes wary as he held her, traces of fear fading from them. Her soft frame was pressed up against him, her full breasts crushed to his chest. He felt a slight stirring of lust but tamped it down. "Are you all right?"

Diana took a deep breath when he let her go, Raphael keeping just a hand on her forearm to keep her steady. He could see she was breathing heavily, as though she were struggling to catch her breath. And now that whatever had threatened her was gone, she was trembling.

Realizing that she wasn't okay, at least not emotionally, he guided her out of the parking deck. He slipped his sunglasses back on. Though not very effective, it was better than nothing to disguise who he was as a few employees came out of the building and headed for their cars. He nodded to a few of them as they passed by. Seeing a bench nearby, he steered her toward it.

"Just take some deep breaths and try to slow your breathing." Raphael took a seat next to her, giving her the time she needed to calm down.

Diana did as he said and managed to get her breathing slow enough to speak, and her heart rate was almost back to normal. "I suppose I should thank you."

He ignored that. "Who was he?"

"Would you believe me if I said an ex-boyfriend?"

Raphael shook his head. "I might have if you hadn't prefaced it that way."

Diana looked up at him, but his eyes were hidden by the dark shades. "He was looking for my father."

"And?"

Diana looked away. "I told him what I told you. He's out of the country."

Raphael grunted. "Guessing he didn't buy that story any more than I did."

She didn't touch that one. "What are you doing here? You don't own Cabotage yet."

Raphael still wasn't sure why he'd come. He'd filed formal papers today. His office had been fielding questions most of the afternoon. Even his uncle had called him. But his uncle knew well why he was taking Lanford down. He applauded him for it. Adeline, however, did not. She, too, had heard the news today. She had been angry when she called. But nothing, not even his sister, was going to stop him from taking away from Lanford everything he cared about. Diana would be the next piece. She just didn't know it yet.

"Well?" Diana clutched her briefcase to her chest.

Raphael shook his head. "I wanted to see you."

Diana rose. "You don't strike me as the type to come all this way to gloat. What do you really want?"

"For now, I'll settle for walking you to your car."

Diana wasn't buying it. "What, you're not going to try to proposition me again?"

Raphael kept pace beside her. "Not today."

Diana unlocked her car and tossed her briefcase across to the passenger seat. "Meaning you will again. Don't hold your breath."

Raphael admired the length of her leg as she slid into the driver's seat and took off his sunglasses. He held the door open. This time his eyes held hers, his tone serious. "Why fight me, Diana? You know you'll lose."

"Why make it easy for you?" Diana tugged on the door, and he let her close it. She backed out of the parking space. She glanced at him once more, then sped out of the parking deck.

Raphael frowned as she stopped and then pulled out onto the busy road. He admired her spunk, but fighting him would be useless. Perhaps if Lanford had come out of hiding sooner, there would have been a chance. And he supposed she had options. She could merge with someone else before he could complete the takeover. But he couldn't see Lanford doing that any more than conceding defeat to him. But Raphael wasn't worried. The goal wasn't to take over Cabotage but to take it from Lanford.

But whatever the compulsion was that drove him to see her today, he was glad he came. Her fear had been very real. Whoever that man was, he wasn't a friend. Raphael knew Lanford had enemies. And Raphael was a firm believer in the phrase "the enemy of my enemy is my friend." He'd been courting relationships with several people who all wanted to see Lanford's demise. Some of those men for reasons as personal as his own. Adeline wasn't the first young woman Lanford seduced. And unfortunately, she wasn't the last.

But something about this situation didn't sit right. Raphael admitted he had less than honorable intentions toward Diana, but he would never harm her. He glanced around one last time to see if he could spot the man who had scared her. It was quiet; most people had already left for the night. He went back to his car, his thoughts back on Diana. He'd see her again Saturday night; she just didn't know it yet.

* * *

Diana sipped her champagne as she strolled the perimeter of the party. Ultimately, she ignored Brett's advice and put the red dress back in her closet and chose a demurer dress. It hugged her figure, but not as much skin on her chest and back was exposed, and the dress went past her knees. She needed Mr. Chambers to listen to her, not ogle her breasts.

She was making her third stroll around the room when she stopped in her tracks. Raphael was standing in a group of men; one of them was Gilbert Chambers. She scowled when he lifted his glass of champagne in her direction. She was contemplating brazenly breaking up the conversation when Raphael spoke to his companions and headed her way.

"Good evening, Diana." Raphael tapped his glass to

hers.

"Figures you'd be here. Don't you have some other unsuspecting company to take over tonight?"

Raphael finished his drink. "Besides your father's, you mean? Nope, not tonight."

"What were you saying to Mr. Chambers?"

Raphael took the glass Diana was strangling in her fingers, setting it aside before she snapped the delicate stem. "Dance with me, and I'll tell you."

Diana wasn't given a chance to protest. Raphael cupped her elbow and firmly led her to where a few other couples were dancing. She glimpsed the snake tattoo as he took her hand firmly in his.

Raphael saw where her eyes were focused. "Snakes are amazing creatures. In old and middle kingdom Egyptian mythology, snakes were associated with immortality. Even today they're seen as symbols of rebirth and renewal."

Diana looked up into Raphael's eyes. His gaze was dark as he watched her face. "Did you get that tattoo before or after prison?"

Raphael's hand tightened on hers for a brief moment, as did the rest of him. Then he made a conscious effort to relax. "Before. I had other things besides rebirth and renewal on my mind when I was released."

Diana shivered. "Revenge. I wonder if you'll find those things after you've succeeded. Something tells me you won't."

"I already have those things. I'm a successful businessman now. Prison was long ago, and hardly anyone knows or cares. The circumstances of my incarceration were well known. And people know what your father did. It was a small price to pay."

Diana looked away. "Somehow, I doubt it was a small price. Perhaps the better word is worthwhile. You promised to tell me what you were saying to Mr. Chambers."

"I was assuring him there would be nothing to worry about when I take over Cabotage. I don't want him to take his account somewhere else. He was your biggest account."

She didn't like the way he emphasized "was." But he was right. If she didn't get Chambers to agree to renew his contract, others would follow suit. "And just when did you tell him that would be?"

"That's going to depend on you. Give it up, Diana. You can't win."

Diana tried to pull away, but Raphael's arm tightened around her waist. "Three months, that's all I'm asking."

Raphael brought her closer. "I heard your reasons. You'll forgive me if your words didn't move me."

Diana kept her voice low, but her words were laced with anger. "I doubt much could. I'm asking you again to give me the time."

"And I ask again, what is in it for me?"

Diana shivered as his fingers stroked her waist through her dress. "You want sex? Fine. I'll give it to you in three months. In exchange, you leave Cabotage alone until then."

Raphael's fingers stopped in their tracks. "I never said I wanted sex, Diana. Though you are quite tempting. Make no mistake. A man would have to be blind or dead to turn you down. I said I wanted you. I didn't say I wanted sex from you. And we both know you have no intention of keeping that bargain."

No, she didn't. Under other circumstances, Raphael Rouillard would have been a temptation. But when those three months were up, she wanted to be long gone. Her father's condition was deteriorating rapidly. She doubted she'd need all three months. More likely just one. This morning he hadn't recognized her for almost two hours, and most of what he had said made no sense. Whatever thoughts or memories had been going through his mind had been terrible. He'd shouted incoherently at the wall for almost an hour. It had disturbed her as much as it had frightened her.

Diana swallowed her nerves. "What exactly do you mean when you say you want me, then?"

Raphael released her as the song ended. "That wasn't part of the bargain. Give Chambers a shot, if you like. It won't matter. Even if you manage to hang onto your clients, and even if you fill every order, it will only delay the inevitable."

Diana stood staring after him as he walked away from her. She cursed under her breath. She looked around. She spotted Chambers. Putting on her best smile and professional façade, she made her way to where he was chatting with a different group of people.

She waited until he acknowledged her before introducing herself. "Mr. Chambers. It's so nice to meet you in person. I'm Diana Kennedy. Lanford's daughter."

"Miss Kennedy. I assumed you'd make an appearance tonight."

Diana stood patiently while he introduced her to the group. "I was hoping we could chat this evening."

Chambers politely dismissed the group. "Perhaps we should talk in my office."

Diana followed Chambers as he wove his way through the throngs of people enjoying his party. When he gestured for her to precede him, she entered the large room. "I appreciate your taking time out to speak with me."

Chambers waved that away, shutting the door behind him. "I already told your people I won't be renewing my contract. Your father has insulted a lot of people with his disappearing act. And leaving his daughter in charge doesn't bolster our confidence."

Diana nodded. "I completely understand your concerns. And I expect when my father returns, he'll address all of them. But Cabotage is ready and able to complete our orders with you. I'll even give you a shorter-term contract."

Chambers poured a drink and swallowed it in one shot. "I was friends with your father some years ago; did you know that?"

Diana wasn't sure why it mattered, but answered. "No. I didn't know."

"Mr. Rouillard seems quite certain the company will be his in a matter of weeks, if not days. He says if I hold out a little longer, we can negotiate a deal that will benefit both of us. There is no reason to negotiate a deal with you, now is there?"

Diana realized for the first time that Chambers was quite drunk. He stumbled a bit as he took a step toward her.

"I can better whatever deal Mr. Rouillard is offering. You say you were a friend of my father's. Then you know how much the company means to him."

Chambers threw the glass he was holding across the room. "I said we were friends. Not that we are. That bastard slept with my wife. She left me after their affair."

Diana took a step back. She didn't like the look in his eyes. "I'm sorry, I didn't know. I'm sure he was sorry for it."

"Yeah, so he said. But I was under contract with him. We have the same friends. He had the nerve to pretend none of it ever happened when we ran into each other. When I threatened him and went to take my business elsewhere, that bastard threatened to sue me. He screws my wife, then he screws me. But you know what, now I can return the favor and screw his daughter."

Diana tried to dodge him, but he was quicker than she had anticipated. The momentum of his body weight as he fell on her took them both to the floor. She tried to struggle under him, but he outweighed her, his gut crushing her to the floor. She tried to scream, but he slapped her before she could make a sound. Though there wasn't much force behind his arm, she felt the inside of her lip split, and her head jerked.

Chambers grabbed the bodice of her dress and tried to tear it. Unsuccessful, he got up on his knees and got a better grip on the fabric until it finally tore.

Diana held still for a moment, biding her time. When his head was inches from her breast, she punched him as hard as she could against the top of his nose. He grunted, and she managed to smash her knee into his groin.

Chambers rolled onto his side, clutching his groin.

Diana looked at the door, but Chambers was between her and it and already getting to his knees. She fled to the other side of the room where there was a window. Chambers tried to get up but dropped back to the floor as she opened the window, kicked the screen loose, and climbed out. As she turned to drop down, she could see his mouth moving, but his words were inaudible. Diana figured it was best she didn't know what he was trying to say. She got halfway across the lawn when she realized she didn't have her purse. She had tucked it in the spare bedroom with everyone else's personal belongings. Trying to slow her breathing and think straight, she stared at the house. She didn't want to go back in.

Diana took a few moments to compose herself when Chambers didn't try to follow her. There wasn't any commotion inside the house that made her believe he had told anyone what had happened. Or at least his perverted side of the story. She glanced down and realized her left breast was hanging out of the dress. The dress had a lining, so she wasn't wearing a bra. She held the fabric across her chest as she made her way back toward the house, her heels sinking into the grass as she went. Her chances of getting back into the party through the front door without being seen were zero, but perhaps she could find some other way inside.

She went around the side of the house where she thought the window to the bedroom was. She tried to open it with one hand, but it didn't budge. Frustrated she looked around for something to smash the glass.

"Now that's an interesting way to try to get that contract."

Diana froze. She didn't need to even hear his voice to know that Raphael was behind her. She could feel his presence. She kept her back to him. "I need my purse."

Raphael came closer and grabbed her arm. When she tried to pull away from him, he spun her around. It was dark on the side of the house, so it was hard to see her face. Her hand was clutching the front of her dress, her hair was disheveled, and her mouth was swollen.

Diana started trembling. "I need my purse."

Raphael let her go, disgust in his voice. "So did you get the contract? You really will sleep with anyone, won't you? Even a fat bastard like Chambers who's old enough to be your father. Like father, like daughter. Guess you had something I couldn't offer."

Diana, already feeling abused, launched herself at him. "You son of a bitch!"

Raphael managed to deflect her blows. He absorbed the weak punches she aimed at his chest. He caught her in his arms. "Enough."

Diana went limp, her energy spent, her left arm still clutching the dress. "Let me go."

Raphael wrapped his arms around her, half dragging her toward the front of the house. As he got closer to the front door, the porch light illuminated her face. He stopped in his tracks. He could see her lip was swelling and there was blood; her hair was more than disheveled, and her dress was torn. "I'll kill him."

Diana was suddenly free. She realized Raphael was

headed for the front door. She ran after him, releasing her dress so she could wrap her arms around him from behind. "Don't! He didn't hurt me, at least not the way you think."

Raphael tried to shake her off, but she suddenly had the strength to hold him. "Let me go, Diana."

Diana tried to reason with him. "You already have a record. If you go in there and attack him, you're the one they'll arrest. Please. Don't."

Raphael took a deep breath. Laughter from inside the house made him realize he couldn't go tearing into the house in front of all those witnesses and attack their host. He patted her hands and pried them from his waist. He turned. "All right. You're right."

Diana closed her eyes, then was startled when she felt his hands closing the front of her dress again. She opened her eyes, blushing suddenly from the embarrassment of him seeing her breast.

"Come on." Raphael fished his car keys from his pocket. He had parked a couple of blocks over. When they got to his car, he opened the passenger door. "What does your purse look like?"

Diana didn't even argue, but simply slipped into the seat. "It's a red beaded bag. Small. It has my keys, my phone, and my license in it."

Raphael lifted Diana's legs into the car and handed her his keys. "I'll be right back."

Diana closed her eyes when Raphael closed the door after hitting the lock button.

* * *

Raphael made his way back to the house, knowing Diana would be safe waiting for him in his car. It was now fully dark out, but the street lamps and lights from the other houses lit the way. He'd gone outside for a breath of fresh air when he heard a noise coming from the side of his host's house. Boredom and curiosity had him looking for the source of the sound. He'd been shocked to see Diana standing in the shadows, looking disheveled. He knew she had gone with Chambers to discuss business. It never occurred to him that Chambers might have something else in mind.

Despite the busted lip, she seemed unhurt, though he was still tempted to find their host and beat the pulp out of him. Instead, he heeded Diana's advice. No one paid much attention to him when he reentered the home. He headed toward the bedroom. The bed was covered in jackets and purses. There was only one red beaded bag on the bed. Just to be sure, he looked inside. Diana's picture on her license looked up at him. He took out her car keys and put them in his trouser pocket. He then pulled out his cell phone. He made a quick call to Kevin, who groggily agreed to meet him.

He saw Chambers talking with the same group of gentlemen he'd been with earlier and didn't notice Raphael glaring at him. Again, it was tempting, but Raphael made his way toward the front door. He nodded at a few acquaintances on the sidewalk and went back to his car. He let out a sigh of relief when Diana was where he'd left her. He knocked on the window.

Startled, Diana's eyes shot to the window. Seeing it was Raphael, she unlocked and opened the door. "Did you find it?"

Raphael handed Diana the purse. He then stripped off his suit jacket and handed it to her. Surprise showed in her eyes, but she took it from him. He turned his back so Diana could release the death grip she had on the front of her dress and put his jacket on without an audience.

Grateful, she hurried and pulled on the suit jacket. It hung on her, but she was able to easily wrap it around her chest. She then opened her purse. "My keys are gone."

Raphael pulled them from his pocket and dangled them out of reach. "I've got them."

Diana went to grab them from him, but he slipped them back into his pocket. "I want my keys."

Raphael closed the car door and came around. He slipped into the driver's seat and held out his hand for the keys he'd given to her. He noticed her reluctance when she handed them over. "You're not driving yourself home."

Diana let out another brief spurt of anger. "I am not leaving my car."

Raphael shrugged. "I had a feeling you would make a fuss."

Diana crossed her arms over her chest as he started the engine and pulled out onto the street. "My car is in the other direction."

Raphael glanced at her. "I'm not kidnapping you. Relax. My brother-in-law is going to meet us at the gas station. He'll drive your car and I'll drive you home."

Diana relaxed, but just a little. "I don't need you to

drive me home. I'm a grown woman."

She hadn't looked like one, Raphael thought. Once he'd gotten a good look at her, she hadn't looked much older than Paul. Her eyes had been wide and frightened, her lips had been trembling, and the hair loose around her face had added to the impression of youth. His sister had worn a similar look after the guilty verdict had come down, and he'd been taken into custody.

Diana was quiet until they were parked in the back of the gas station lot. "You said your brother-in-law was coming?"

"Yes. His name is Kevin. He married Adeline a couple of years ago."

"You didn't need to drag him out of bed. I'm capable of driving myself home."

Raphael looked her over. The fear had faded from her eyes, and she didn't seem dazed anymore. "What happened?"

Diana turned away and flexed her hand. It still hurt from when she punched Chambers. And hitting Raphael's solid chest hadn't helped. "I'm sorry I hit you."

He shrugged it off. "It was justified. What happened?"

"Just another enemy of my father. I suppose he wanted the same thing you did. Revenge and me. Of course, he was willing to take me by force. I can't help but wonder how many more men want the same thing. First, there was you, then that man in the parking deck, threatening calls at all hours, and now Chambers."

Raphael would have spoken, but Diana gave a harsh laugh.

"You know, this is why I left eight years ago. Nothing has changed since. If anything, it's worse."

Raphael gripped the steering wheel, filing away her comment about threatening calls. "Where is your father, Diana?"

She leaned back and closed her eyes. "He's not coming back, Raphael."

Frustrated, he squeezed the wheel under his hands. "That doesn't answer my question."

Diana sighed and snuggled into his jacket. "No, it doesn't."

Seeing her start to relax, Raphael let it go and leaned back in his seat as they waited for Kevin.

Half an hour later, Raphael got out of the car to greet his brother-in-law.

Kevin knew who the woman in the front seat of Raphael's car was. "So want to tell me how it is I'm standing outside a gas station at almost midnight getting ready to drive Diana Kennedy's car home?"

Raphael was wondering that himself. Seeing her cut lip, knowing someone had attacked her, made him forget she was the enemy. He could no more have left her than he could have left his sister. "Gilbert Chambers tried to use Diana as a substitute for her father."

It didn't take much to put two and two together, given what Kevin could see of her face. "So why didn't you call the cops instead of me?"

Raphael's gut clenched. "Let's just say I haven't been a fan of law enforcement or the justice system since my incarceration."

"Yeah, I guess I get that. All right, let's go. Adeline was worried when I left. She's probably pacing the house, wondering what kind of trouble you've gotten yourself into."

Raphael couldn't help but wonder that himself. He had plans to use Diana to gain control of Lanford's business. But he had a nasty feeling those plans were about to go out the window. It had been easy to hate Diana before he'd met her. It had been easy to place part of the blame for what happened to him and his family on her because of her standing beside her father. He didn't like this feeling of empathy toward her at all.

Raphael tossed Kevin Diana's keys. "I don't know. But Adeline needn't worry."

Kevin palmed the keys, his eyes drifting to Diana's still form. "Well, there's worry, and then there's worry."

Raphael shrugged off his odd mood. "Right. Let's get Diana home so Adeline can get some sleep."

Chapter Four

Diana had seen a car drop the man chatting with Raphael off and leave. She'd not even tried to listen in on Raphael's and Kevin's conversation, though she had no doubt she was the topic of conversation. Diana knew about the wedding. She knew almost everything that involved Paul. Diana knew neither Adeline nor Raphael would appreciate her snooping, but like it or not, Paul was her half-brother. She loved Nick and Drew. She'd been thrilled when they'd been born. And she loved her stepsister Shandy as if she were blood. It hurt that she had another brother but only knew facts about his life. But she had not wanted to intrude on Adeline or Paul. Her father had hurt both of them enough. Diana didn't want to add to that hurt. She had a private investigator who discreetly sent her pictures and an update on him once a year.

She was curious about the man who was helping raise Paul. He had similar coloring and build to Raphael but was several inches shorter. The man had been looking at her through the windshield; she could see his surprise when he saw her in the passenger seat. He obviously knew who she was. Diana barely stirred when Raphael got back in the car, and she didn't turn when Kevin slipped into the back seat.

She gave Raphael the intersection where she'd left her car parked. She was so tired, and despite Raphael's and Kevin's presence, she felt safe. For a brief moment, tucked away in Raphael's car, wearing Raphael's jacket, she felt a reprieve. For a few moments, she could forget what Chambers had tried to do, could forget Raphael was trying to take over her father's company, could forget Raphael was her enemy, and could forget her father was sick. She could set aside her worry for her brothers' futures and simply let her mind drift.

Diana watched without much interest as Kevin climbed into her car and followed them to her condo building. She did sit up, though, as Raphael drove through the mostly empty streets. When they pulled up in front of her condo, she sat for a moment, trying to think of what she should say. Thank you didn't seem enough.

"I'll walk you up."

That got Diana's attention. "No. I'm fine."

Raphael halted her as she started to take off the jacket. "Keep it. I'll be seeing you again."

Though it didn't necessarily sound like a threat, Diana took it as one. She hurriedly climbed from the car. She looked up into Kevin's face as she held her hand out for her keys. He had kind eyes, and she saw nothing but sympathy there. When he dropped her keys into her palm, she smiled. "Thanks. And sorry you had to come out."

Diana rushed inside, grateful to escape Raphael and his words that he'd be seeing her again. No. It hadn't sounded like a threat, but she knew it was.

* * *

Kevin watched as she made her way quickly to the

entrance of her condo building. He shook his head and climbed into the car. "Pretty lady."

As if Raphael hadn't noticed. "Yeah. Now let's get you home before Adeline works herself up into a panic."

Adeline met them at the door. She hugged her husband and kissed him a bit harder than she intended. "Thank goodness."

Raphael closed the front door behind him. "And what am I?"

Adeline hugged him. "I'm more apt to box your ears. What happened? Kevin said you sounded cryptic on the phone."

Kevin yawned and hugged his wife to his side. "We rescued a damsel in distress. Wait until you hear who."

Adeline could only think of one person. "What did you do, Raph? I told you to leave Diana Kennedy alone."

Raphael scowled at his sister. "Did you hear the damsel in distress part? Diana got herself into a bit of a situation. I was there and I helped."

"Don't you think for one second I believe that. I wasn't an innocent victim, Raphael, no matter what you think. I was young, but I knew what I was doing; what he wanted. I admit I fell for Lanford's charm, but at no point did he hurt me physically. Let it go. You wouldn't have been anywhere near her tonight if you hadn't been bent on revenge because of me."

Raphael felt a twinge of guilt. Diana most likely would not have found herself in that situation if he hadn't been there. He knew deep down his presence, and his riling Chambers up with his promise of a better contract, contributed to Chambers's drinking and his assault on Diana. Chambers consumed one glass of whiskey after another while raging on about Lanford's affair with his wife, all while Raphael pretended sympathy. He had listened and nodded while Chambers had started in on how he was practically being blackmailed by Lanford. By the time Diana had sought him out, he'd been well and truly angry. And he'd attempted to take that fury out on Diana.

Raphael kissed his sister's cheek. "Then I'll do it for me. Lanford did everything in his power to play the victim of a brutal attack. And while it was tempting, and while I am guilty of punching the man, I didn't try to kill him. Two and a half years, Adeline, he took from me. You don't want me doing this because of you. Fine. I'll do it for me."

Adeline hated to see that distant look in Raphael's eyes on the rare times he mentioned his time in jail. "And Diana?"

Raphael remembered the look on Diana's face. "I won't hurt her. I promise. I think we can make a satisfactory deal. She wants something from me, and in return, I can protect her from the fallout and her father's enemies. Happy?"

Adeline held out her hand. She and her brother always shook hands when they made a deal. She smiled when he reluctantly took her hand. "I am now."

* * *

Diana managed to get some sleep Saturday night. It wasn't much, but it had been better than nothing. Sunday Jasmine took the day off, so other than her father, she had been alone in the condo. She had spent some time tidying up the place, cleaning up the kitchen, doing some laundry, and trying to work off some of her stress. She glanced at her paints, sketch pad, and canvases stacked against the wall. Her fingers didn't itch to pick them up. She hadn't painted much of anything since the day she'd gone back to Cabotage.

She'd spent all day Monday expecting Raphael to show up. Instead, the office had been quiet, and he hadn't made the promised visit. Of course, he hadn't said when they would see each other again, only that they would.

Tuesday had brought some additional bad news. Her father's rival, Benjamin Houghton, was circling behind Raphael, most likely looking to see what he could salvage from the remains of her father's business when Raphael was through with it. As far as she knew, Ben owned a few shares, so he had likely been in touch with Raphael to see what he could do to help the business's demise.

Ben had been her father's friend when Lanford had been married to her mother, Julianne. He was also her godfather. He used to give her the most exquisite dolls for her birthday. She still remembered how hard she'd cried when her father had tossed them all out. Despite the fallout, Ben had still sent her a birthday card throughout her childhood years, and neither of them bore any ill will toward the other. Despite her father's objections, she'd stayed in touch with Ben, and now that she was older, she thought of Ben as a good friend.

If anyone knew what type of man Lanford was, Ben did. She had been contemplating seeking his help, but she knew it wasn't fair to drag him into this. Lanford had tried to destroy Ben's company, thankfully unsuccessfully. Ben had helped Julianne when she'd decided to leave her husband. For a time, Ben was the only man who knew where she'd gone.

By Wednesday afternoon, Diana was so stressed she almost wished Raphael would show up. His jacket was folded and sitting on a table in the corner of her office. It was an unwelcome reminder of what had taken place Saturday night. She was having a hard time getting rid of the feel of Chamber's body on top of hers. And the memory was not helping her sleep at night.

On top of that, Diana was still trying to put the incident at the parking deck out of her mind, but the memory of the man who had confronted her and the fear she'd felt had yet to completely fade. Security cameras hadn't captured a good shot of him, so she had nothing to take to the police. She had security meet her at her car and walk her back each evening, but the man didn't make another appearance. And since no one else was in danger, she hadn't pressed the issue.

Unfortunately, the phone calls hadn't stopped. She had blocked several numbers so her phone would stop ringing, but because staff and clients had her cell phone number, she couldn't simply change her number. Despite blocking the calls, there had been voicemails left, but none had been overtly threatening. Again, the likelihood of the police taking an active interest was slim.

She was getting ready to call it a day Wednesday afternoon when Brett poked his head into her office. "What's up?"

"Got the latest numbers. Dropped a few more points."

Diana rubbed her brow. "Ok. I expect we'll be hearing from Rouillard any day."

Brett backed out of her office and almost backed into the man behind him. He looked up. "Well, speak of the devil. Ms. Kennedy, you've got a guest."

Diana rose from her seat, her eyes on Raphael. She saw him look the older man over, then dismiss him.

Raphael closed the door behind him in the man's face. "You should have warned your staff about me if you wanted to keep me out."

Diana shivered at his cool tone. "I didn't think it would be necessary. And hardly productive anyway. You'd have found a way in. I thought I'd hear from you sooner."

Raphael took a seat, crossing his ankle over his knee. She could see he was taking her in: the fair skin, her long blonde hair once again coiled at her nape, and the blue silk suit that fit her like a glove. "I've had a lot of thinking to do. And I've been thinking about the three months you asked me for. And what I might want in exchange. I've decided what I want."

Diana set her pen down. "I have a counterproposal."

Raphael raised a black brow at her. "You haven't heard what I want yet."

"I heard enough the last time I was in your office. I've been thinking, too. What if I told you I could sell you my father's shares in three months?"

"Ah, the magic number again. All right, I'll bite. First, what makes you think you can get your hands on your father's shares? I figure the only way you'll get a hold of them is to pry them from his cold, dead hands."

Diana stiffened at how close he'd inadvertently come to the truth. "I can't tell you how. I just can. Then I'll sell them to you. It's the best choice for everyone. Lanford will no longer control Cabotage, and the business stays intact for the people who work here. I think deep down you care that you'd be hurting innocent people if you destroyed the company."

Raphael shook his head. "If not me, it will be someone else. Rumors are Ben Houghton is sniffing around. I spoke with him about selling me his shares. Right now he's holding out to see what I'm going to do, but there's no doubt he's next in line if I change my mind. And why should I buy what I'll be able to take?"

That was the billion-dollar question, wasn't it? There was nothing in it for him. But if he knew her father was dying, he might dump the stock he'd bought, sending the company into even deeper waters. If any more of their investors or clients pulled out, they were done for.

"I'll sell them for ten percent less than their future worth."

Raphael laughed. "No deal. I like my idea better. I've decided what I want. I've decided I do want you."

Diana stood, her cheeks red with anger. "I want you out of my office."

Raphael uncrossed his ankle and got slowly to his feet, keeping his eyes on Diana. "I'm not after your virtue, Diana. I'm after your influence."

Confused, Diana watched his face. "What influence?"

"Have a seat. It's not that complicated. People here

respect you. I've been asking around. Once I take over the company, people are going to be upset and scared for their jobs. And you're right, I'm not interested in destroying anyone's livelihood, other than your father's. And I'm not interested in destroying the business. I'm interested in taking it away from Lanford, and I won't be stopped. It's the only thing he cares about. I've decided you're going to help me."

She sat back down. "What else?"

He appeared to think about it for a moment. "You are right, though. I wouldn't be opposed to getting my hands on your father's shares. But I don't need them. He doesn't own enough of them to keep control of the company or the power to stop me. Here's my proposal. If you get your hands on his shares, I'll give you the face value of what they are worth today. If you don't get a hold of them, you cooperate with me anyway, and I owe you nothing."

Diana felt a little bit of her tension fade. "All you want is my cooperation?"

Raphael smiled, but it wasn't reassuring. "It will be a little more than just your cooperation, but we'll get to that in a moment. Deal?"

Diana thought about today's value of those shares. She hoped that in three months their value would increase when she sold them. She hadn't seen the numbers, but since Brett just told her their value was down again, she had a pretty good idea of what they were worth right now. And it wasn't enough. "Today's face value plus twenty-five percent."

"Twenty."

Diana nodded. It had to be enough. "Cooperation and

what?"

Raphael stayed standing as he watched her face. "The best way to get what I want is simple. I want you to be my wife."

Diana paled. Her voice was a squeak. "Wife?"

Raphael pulled two contracts out of his briefcase. "A prenuptial agreement. And a business contract. I don't trust you to keep your word. We'll have to modify them a little to include you selling me the shares, assuming you get them."

Her fingers were numb as she took the papers from him. "Why wife? Why not fiancée, or girlfriend, or lover?"

Raphael went back to his explanation. "A few reasons. Having you as my wife will make it seem as if Lanford has given his blessing. The staff will congratulate you, the shareholders will be pleased, and business can go on as usual. No hostile takeover necessary. A friendly merger, if you will."

Since he'd said the word wife, she had been running through her mind what that might mean. And how it might benefit her, too. Diana thought of her father back at her condo. If she agreed to Raphael's plan, she could simply say her father had turned over the day-to-day operations to her husband. Semi-retirement so-to-speak. Then when the shares were hers, she could sell them quickly to Raphael before announcing her father's death. There were no friends, no family, waiting in the wings to swoop in upon his death. If she were careful, and if she timed it right, she'd have the money in hand before Raphael knew she had deceived him. He'd have his revenge, though it would be tepid at best. And as soon as the announcement was made, she could be on a plane. The divorce might be a tricky proposition, but since she didn't plan to get married, he could take as much time as he liked divorcing her.

Diana glanced at the contract, weighing her decision carefully. She read through the documents. When she was done, she looked up at him. "Adjust the contract so it states you'll pay face value plus twenty percent, and I'll sign."

"Consider it done."

"I have other conditions."

Raphael tapped his finger on the contract. "I have no doubt. I'm not an unreasonable man."

Unreasonable? No, perhaps not. But she was still perplexed. "I still don't understand why you insist on marriage. It seems a little extreme for you to marry someone you despise."

He didn't argue the point, though the anger he had felt toward her had faded. He shrugged. "It will simplify things."

Diana set the contract in front of her. "I won't sleep with you. I won't let you tell my brothers this isn't a real marriage. I expect to live under the same roof. And I expect the money deposited the minute I have the shares in hand. Once I have the money and you have the shares, I expect a quiet divorce. No need to make a spectacle of it."

Raphael took a good look at her defiant face. "That's it?"

Diana nodded. "That's it."

Raphael took the contracts back from her. "I'll have them redrawn and sent over. I'll arrange the wedding for

Saturday. But, Diana, the marriage will last six months regardless of the shares or the money. I'll need time to stabilize the business. I can't save the company from the damage your father did if you're not committed to this."

Diana figured that once he knew of her deceit, he'd grant her an early divorce, no matter where she was. "Done."

Raphael tucked the papers back into his briefcase. "And your father?"

"I'll deliver the happy news if he happens to call. Don't forget your jacket."

Raphael didn't like the look in Diana's eyes, but he let it go. He'd gotten what he wanted. And surprisingly, without much persuasion. He was looking forward to the confrontation with Lanford. And Raphael had no doubt that his marrying Lanford's daughter and taking the company from him would have the old man back on the first flight home from wherever he was hiding.

He grabbed his jacket on the way out.

Diana closed her eyes and rubbed her brow as soon as Raphael had closed the door behind him. She certainly hadn't expected Raphael to show up and propose marriage. She wasn't sure if she should laugh or cry. But if the company stayed afloat, a hostile takeover prevented, and if she could get the focus off her father's absence and onto Raphael, then she'd consider the plan a success. But she also knew she would have to be careful and not tip her hand. And she wasn't sure how she was going to explain this to her brothers. They might be younger than her, but they were very protective. They saw her as being somewhat delicate, not world savvy. And given her track record with men, she couldn't say she blamed them for thinking she was naive.

But Diana also wondered if Raphael had considered what his sister and nephew might think. But Diana also wondered if perhaps she might have the opportunity to get to know them, or at least, they might get to know her so they could decide if they wanted to pursue a relationship after she divorced Raphael. It would be impossible to keep their marriage a secret. Society pages were bound to speculate about the haste of their marriage. They were already speculating where Lanford Kennedy might be hiding. Business pages would be speculating if the marriage was a desperate attempt by Diana to save the company. It was common knowledge in the business community that Raphael and Lanford were enemies. And since Raphael had already filed papers to take the company over, speculation as to their sudden marriage would run rampant.

But if the company could be brought back from the brink, Raphael could do it. In the ten years since he'd been released from prison and had gone to work for his uncle, Rouillard Enterprises had thrived. For Raphael, Cabotage would be just another acquisition in an already full portfolio. For Diana and those who remained, he could secure their futures.

* * *

Raphael was more than satisfied as he closed Diana's office door behind him and made his way out of Cabotage's office. People were staring at him, but he ignored them. They'd eventually get used to seeing him around.

The conversation had gone much as he had hoped. He had answered Diana's question as to why he wanted to marry her, but he had yet to answer the question to himself with any level of satisfaction. Raphael had originally intended to fake a romantic relationship between them. He certainly hadn't intended to legally tie himself to Lanford's daughter. Part of the reason for the marriage was his promise to Adeline. If he was to keep that promise to his sister, and in turn keep Diana safe, he doubted a fake engagement, or a fake affair, would be sufficient. He still wasn't sure when the idea of marrying her had come to him, possibly while lying awake in bed unable to sleep, remembering the length of her legs and the glimpse he'd gotten of her breast. But once the idea had taken root, he decided it was the best way. He'd get her cooperation, he'd see to her safety by stowing her away at his home, and he could ensure the company transitioned smoothly as Rouillard Enterprises consumed it. He'd have achieved his objective while making Adeline happy.

And while he believed marriage was a serious matter and should be for life, he'd broken many other rules in his lifetime; this would just be one more. So while he wasn't convinced of his motives, or whether this truly was the only way, the plan was now in motion, and he wasn't regretting it.

He had enjoyed watching the different emotions pass on Diana's beautiful face when he told her he wanted to marry her. And it didn't get past him that having a woman like Diana Kennedy as a wife could also be to his professional benefit. As he had told her earlier, people did like and respect her. People might not like her father; some even hated him, but it was not only the employees at Cabotage who spoke fondly of her. A few clients and investors he had met had as well. People tolerated Lanford while his business was profitable. Now that it was failing, they were not so tolerant. But many expressed their surprise and approval at her sudden return to the company.

Time would tell if he had made the right decision, or if he'd only been acting on a moment of lust that he'd come to regret.

Chapter Five

It didn't take long for Diana to empty her personal belongings and painting supplies from her condo and pack them up in a U-Haul. She had already stored her completed paintings in a climate-controlled rental locker, along with the art that belonged to her father, which would be hers when he was gone.

She planned to turn the condo over to a real estate agent as soon as Lanford was gone, and she had decided to sell the furniture and most of the stuff with it. She didn't want Raphael anywhere near her condo to help her move furniture or any of her belongings, so she only packed what she would take with her when she left California. She had artist friends in New York who had been trying to convince her to move for years. She hadn't called them yet but knew they would help her navigate her way around the city when she got there.

Raphael had called her a couple of times since Wednesday, and they had met only long enough to get their marriage license. There was a small chapel that promised same-day marriages not far from where he worked, and Diana had agreed to meet him there on Saturday morning. She had informed him that her stepmother and brothers would be there. He had been silent for a time but then simply said, "Fine."

It had taken quite a bit of fast-talking to convince

Larissa that she wasn't being forced or coerced into the marriage. She explained that she and Raphael had spent some time together, and given the delicate state of the business, decided that marriage was the best course of action. Larissa had been less than satisfied, but Diana wasn't a child and could make her own decisions.

As for her brothers, well, they were easy to convince. She told them she'd gotten to know Raphael well and that the past was water under the bridge. Nick and Drew knew the business was struggling, but they couldn't care less. When Diana told them it was a wedding present, that Raphael was buying her shares, and that they would now be able to go to Berkeley as they'd planned, they were ecstatic and that was the end of the discussion. They wanted to check him out but were pleased she had chosen such a successful and generous man for a husband.

Diana hadn't even blinked when she'd told the lie that she'd sold her shares to Raphael. Despite working for Lanford, she had never held any shares. But she certainly wasn't ever going to tell them that. Seeing the joy on their identical faces had been all she needed to see to confirm she was doing the right thing. Both boys were heavily into math and science, and Berkeley offered them excellent opportunities to boost their careers. She could picture both of them working for NASA or some giant think tank one day. If all she had to do was hold out until Lanford passed and marry her father's enemy, then it was a small price to pay to see them succeed.

Friday afternoon, she stood in front of the board and announced her plans to marry Raphael Rouillard. She hinted at a long-term affair and that the papers had gotten it wrong. Raphael was not the enemy as everyone thought. She just wanted to keep the affair private. But since they were getting married, she wanted the truth to come out. Diana wasn't sure how much of the story they believed, especially given the emergency meeting they'd had about the takeover and how they might stop it, but she didn't care. Brett had been stunned, and she could see speculation in his eyes. But he didn't contradict her, so no one else did either. After that, she'd locked herself in her office until it was time for security to escort her out.

So here she was on a beautiful, sunny Saturday afternoon about to get married. She had never thought she would get married, but she took the commitment she was making seriously. She had taken time off work and bought a not-quite-white suit with eyelet details on the cuffs and hem of the jacket and skirt. She'd paired it with a pale blue satin blouse. She also decided to wear her grandmother's pearl earrings and necklace and a pair of delicate silver-heeled sandals. She had swept up her hair and left soft tendrils loose around her face and neck. She had finished the look with fake baby's breath woven into the pinned tresses.

When she stepped inside the small chapel, she could see the surprise on Raphael's face. And it didn't get past her notice when he'd looked her over from top to toe. She had a brother on each arm. Raphael was standing near the altar with Kevin by his side. He had also dressed for the occasion. The suit was a dark gray, similar to the one he'd been wearing the day she'd confronted him in his office, though this one had a slight sheen to it. The dress shirt was almost the same blue as the blouse she chose. A dark, discreetly striped tie and black dress shoes finished the look.

She then looked around and saw that his sister, Adeline, was sitting on a pew in the front and was turned her way. It had been years since she'd seen the woman in person. She looked much as she had years before, though she did not seem to be angry or upset, or any other emotion she had expected to see on the face of the woman her father had seduced and gotten pregnant all those years ago. She seemed almost pleased by the events unfolding.

When she got to the front of the chapel, Adeline rose to stand by her husband.

Raphael was the first to speak. "When you said your family was coming, I felt I should do the same. Diana, my sister, Adeline."

Adeline held out a hand. "It's nice to meet you, Diana."

Diana found she couldn't speak. She took the woman's hand and squeezed it.

Adeline could see the question in her eyes. "I didn't bring him."

Diana told herself to get a grip. "I'm sorry. I just...I didn't think you'd be here."

Adeline tucked her arm back in her husband's. "I wasn't sure if I should come or not. But if my brother is marrying you, we can't pretend the past never happened. I'm a strong believer in confronting awkward situations and getting them out of the way. Depending on how your marriage goes, we'll see about my son."

She nodded in understanding. "These are my brothers,

Nick and Drew. And their mother, Larissa."

Larissa shook Raphael's hand first. "We're grateful to you for what you've done."

Diana could tell Raphael was not sure what Larissa meant and was grateful when he kept quiet. Raphael, Kevin, and Adeline took turns shaking the boy's hands. The twins had been eyeing him since they had come in. Standing next to Raphael, Diana couldn't help but notice again how young the twins still were and how much they needed her.

Nick, the ringleader of the two, looked Raphael over. "Guess you'll do. You look a sight better than her last boyfriend."

Diana turned red. "Seriously, you two. He wasn't that bad."

Drew disagreed. "Guy was a wimp. Couldn't handle Di's success. A real weenie. Do you really own a corporation?"

Raphael smiled at the two young men. "I do. And I promise not to let Diana intimidate me."

The boys nodded. Nick spoke again. "Anyway, like Mom said, we can't thank you enough for buying Di's shares. We were both accepted at Berkeley, but we weren't sure we were going to get to go. Mom is still going to go to Philadelphia to stay with our other sister, Shandy, but we're grateful we get to stay. So thank you."

This time, Raphael glanced at Diana.

Diana ignored the question in his eyes. "I'm ready when you are."

The first thing Raphael did was gesture to the contracts on a nearby table. She glanced up at him again, but then lowered her lashes. Her brothers had released her arms when they shook Raphael's hand. She took the pen he handed her. Taking a deep breath and holding it, she signed first the prenuptial contract and then the business one. She let her breath out slowly. She watched Raphael as he boldly signed them.

Raphael turned to Adeline. "We'll need witnesses."

Adeline signed, then Larissa signed.

A short man with a shaved head and a white robe gestured for them to come to the altar.

The vows were traditional ones. Diana was glad Raphael had chosen the small chapel instead of a judge's chambers. And while the courthouse might have made this feel less real, for the sake of both their families, it was better this way.

She trembled slightly when Raphael kissed her, but otherwise, she didn't let on to the new set of nerves that settled in her belly. For better or for worse, she had just married Raphael Rouillard.

They then signed their wedding certificate, with Adeline and Larissa once again witnessing it.

Drew hugged her tightly and released her so Nick could do the same. Drew was the more affectionate of the two. She kissed their cheeks with tears in her eyes. If for no other reason than these two young men, she knew she couldn't regret marrying Raphael. Though not how she had imagined it, she had done what she'd set out to do. She wouldn't be able to give Larissa a down payment for the condo she wanted, but at least she could do this for her brothers.

"All right, enough of this mushy stuff. We should go eat." Nick released his sister.

Drew seconded that.

Diana looked over at Raphael. She didn't see victory on his face like she thought she might. Instead, he was smiling at her brothers. Then his eyes turned to hers. She gave him a warm smile. "Yes, let's go eat."

They took the cars they drove in. Kevin and Adeline had come in their own, so they could go straight home. Diana opted to ride with Larissa and her brothers. She thought Raphael might protest, but he'd only nodded as he led her out of the chapel.

The wedding party filled a small room at the back of a family-style restaurant. Diana sat next to Raphael while Kevin and Adeline sat across from them. Larissa sat on the other side of Diana with the boys across from her.

Nick and Drew had no trouble finding things to talk about. It never failed to amuse Diana how in tune they were. Raphael was mostly silent while Adeline attempted to make light conversation, asking a few questions here and there, but never directly referencing the fact that Diana was Lanford Kennedy's daughter and her son's half-sister.

Larissa and the boys were the first to leave. They once again hugged their sister and thanked Raphael for dinner. Kevin and Adeline left shortly after.

Raphael took a sip of his coffee and leaned back in his seat. "Why do your brothers think I paid their college tuition using your shares of Cabotage?"

Diana spun her empty coffee cup between her palms. "I didn't want them to know the truth."

"You said that before, but about the marriage, not the money. College is expensive. Did you think I'd just hand the money over to you?"

Diana sighed. She had hoped they could find even ground, perhaps declare a truce. But her hopes were fading at the look Raphael was giving her. "I took out a loan to cover the down payment for the tuition. They'll need dorm rooms, and the money is due now. I'll get those shares, you'll pay me as promised, I'll pay off the loan, and they'll never know. If I told them I was paying their tuition out of my own money, they'd have rebelled."

Raphael pushed the coffee cup back. "Doesn't sound like kids I know. Most would be happy to take the money as their due, no matter where it came from."

Diana rose, her anger barely suppressed at his insulting tone. "They are not my father. Do you understand? They don't take. They think the money for the shares was a wedding gift, a favor to me. They don't mind taking company money. But if they knew I had paid it with my own, they would have refused to go. They deserve better."

Raphael took Diana's hand. "And what of their sister? Does she deserve better?"

Diana pulled her hand away. "When you decide on the answer to that, let me know. We should go."

They got into another argument when Diana tried to pay the restaurant bill. When she realized that he had no problem arguing or embarrassing her in public, she relented.

She stood outside his white Mercedes sports car as he paid the bill.

Raphael unlocked the door and opened it for her. "Anything else you need from your condo tonight?"

Diana shook her head. "No. I hired a young man from my building to drive the U-Haul I packed to your house tomorrow. I wasn't sure what to do with my things, so I only packed up what I would need for the next six months."

Raphael held the door until she was inside, then closed it. He rounded the car and picked up where they'd left off. "I have plenty of room for your things. I have a den I never use if you have furniture you need to put somewhere."

Diana simply shook her head. He didn't know of her plans to sell the condo and leave California when this was over, nor did she plan to enlighten him. "No sense dragging my entire condo to your home. I doubt you need another sofa or pots and pans. Just my clothes and some things I'd rather not live without."

Diana could tell Raphael was relieved he wasn't going to have to drag all of her things over.

Raphael eased into traffic. "That's fine. The spare bedrooms are quite large, so feel free to fill them with whatever."

They drove quite a way out of town and into an elite neighborhood. She gaped when they pulled up into the driveway of a large, white Spanish-style house. The house sat on three levels, the garage at the base with dark wood doors. A stone walkway led to six steps to the front door that was inset, so an overhang would keep the rain off while opening the door. The slim balcony over the garage drew the eye upwards to the terracotta-tiled roof that contrasted with the whitewashed exterior and black shutters.

"This is beautiful." Diana was so focused on the house that she didn't see Raphael grab her oversized suitcase from the back seat.

"Thanks. Rouillard Enterprises built it."

She smiled at that. "But of course. Your uncle designed this, didn't he?"

His head jerked in her direction. "How did you know that?"

"Basile Rouillard is a genius architect. He loves angles, but they never look harsh. Did he do the interiors too?"

He gestured for her to follow him inside. "I'm surprised you know my uncle's work. He designed a bit of it. He's responsible for the high ceilings and the beams. At the time, all I cared about was an open floor plan. And a big kitchen."

Diana closed the front door behind her. The house immediately opened up into a living area. The furniture fit the Spanish style of the home, and the colors were warm. "I see you like blue."

Raphael set her suitcase down. "I like blue. Come on, I'll show you the rest."

The kitchen was partially closed off from the living room, but a large arched entryway kept the open feeling. Here was a modern kitchen. The dark wood and light quartz counters contrasted yet seemed to blend. The floors were dark wood throughout, but there were plenty of windows to keep the space from being too dark, even in the fading light of the sunset. The fridge was double the size of a standard one, the island bigger than anyone would ever need, and a large dining set was set off to the side, burnished yellows and more blues bringing color into the room.

"You can have your pick of bedrooms." He glanced over, but Diana wasn't following him. "That's my office."

Diana didn't respond; her eyes were fixed on a large painting hanging between two large windows that she could see through the open door. She stepped into the room, heedless of his eyes watching her. It was a moody piece, the fluid lines of the painting concealing yet revealing the subject.

Raphael gestured to the painting she was staring at. "I suppose paintings of the ocean are a bit overdone here in Cali. But I liked this one. And it doesn't hurt that there is a bit of mystery surrounding the artist. No one knows who the artist is. But I think it's a woman."

Diana registered his comment. "A woman? You said no one knows who the artist is."

"You can tell. The painting is all curves and fluid lines. It's very sensuous and very feminine. Her paintings are always signed with an off-center 'D' entwined with an 'E.' When I asked the gallery owner the painter's name, he just said he calls them D's."

Diana realized she was staring at him. He probably thought she was crazy. But when she saw her painting hanging on his wall, she stopped in shock. "You like art?"

Raphael shrugged. "I like this painting. I don't know if I like art for the sake of it."

Diana looked around the large room and saw a couple more paintings on the walls of his office. None of the rest were hers. She gestured to a different painting on the far side of his office. "I love art. I paint. Not as good as that, but it's something I've always done. It's the only thing Lanford and I have in common. When I sold the contents of his house, the paintings were the only things I kept. I put them in storage before the bank inspector came."

"You sold the contents of his house?"

Diana realized what she'd said. She was still awed that he owned one of her paintings that she'd forgotten for a moment her lies. She quickly backtracked. "He's not in the country, remember? Someone had to do it. You already know the bank foreclosed. But before the appraisers started swarming the house, I took the art and sold off a lot of the contents. The bank wasn't going to even try to get top dollar. But the paintings I kept. I figured if nothing else, he owes me that much for managing his affairs while he's away. He had quite the collection, though he sold most of them over the past couple of years. I don't think he truly appreciated them for what they were, though. He was more interested in their value."

Raphael pointed back to the painting that had first grabbed her attention. "That one cost a pretty penny. I'd say the artist isn't starving. But I think the value of a painting is in the eye of the beholder. I doubt your father saw beyond the price tag."

Diana reluctantly left the office and grabbed the handle of her suitcase. "Art was the only thing my father let me have after my mother left. I had a teacher come in once a week during my childhood. Then when I turned sixteen and could drive myself, I found a better teacher. He paid for all of it without a fuss. But he would rage every time I bought clothes or shoes, or some other trinket. I owe him for those lessons, if nothing else."

He took the handle from her and carried the suitcase up the stairs. "I don't know if I'd go that far. I'm sure you've more than repaid him over the years. My room is at the end of the hall. You have three rooms you can choose from. The one on the right is the largest."

Diana took a moment to find her bearings. She chose the door on the left. She smiled in satisfaction. There were large windows, the bed taking up space opposite them. If she moved the dresser, she would be able to set up her easel and get the morning and afternoon light in this room. "I'll take this one."

Raphael raised a brow at her satisfied tone. "You haven't seen the other rooms."

Diana turned and held her hand out for the suitcase handle. "I don't need to see them. I want this one."

"Fine. This one does not have a private bath, like the one across the hall. Your bathroom will be next door, between the two smaller bedrooms."

Diana took the handle he offered and rolled it near the dresser. She left it and crossed the room to the closet. She gave him another satisfied smile. "This will be fine."

Raphael showed her the bathroom that was to be hers and left her to her own devices.

* * *

Raphael went back downstairs. He paused and headed to his office. He stopped and looked at the painting she had been admiring. He shrugged and went to his computer.

Perhaps she did just like art. But her reaction to the painting had been strange, to say the least.

Chapter Six

Sunday morning dawned with plenty of sunshine and a nice warm breeze. Diana stood outside on the deck that was attached to the back of Raphael's house, sipping her coffee. It was still hard to believe she had married Raphael yesterday. His argument had seemed logical, but mostly Diana had seen it as a way to solve a few of her problems. With the nurse on duty at her condo watching over her father, she didn't have to worry about him being alone. She didn't have to sleep on her living room floor on an air mattress. And now she had plenty of time to stall Raphael. She wasn't sure why she believed him when he said he'd pay her the money for her father's shares, but she did, and now she had a signed contract.

Of course, the marriage would cause her a few problems, too. She'd had to hire a second nurse to spend Sundays with her father when Jasmine was off. She had a meeting coming up with the lawyer who was handling her claim to gain power of attorney over her father. There was a competency hearing later in the week. So far, she'd managed to get her father's signatures on all the legal paperwork she'd needed him to sign, but his lucid days were now few and far between. She also needed to start looking into hiring a real estate agent to put her condo on the market. But she could hardly invite someone into her home right now.

But most importantly, once she had the power of attorney papers and the legal right to make decisions for her father, she could start the paperwork that would turn Lanford's shares of Cabotage over to Raphael. And with the money from Raphael, she could make the final payment to the university so her brothers could start in the fall.

Then she could start making plans to start over.

"Such a pensive mood on a beautiful morning."

Diana stiffened for a moment but then told herself to relax. "You've got a beautiful home, Raphael."

He came and stood beside her. "I suppose it's a bit much for a bachelor, but once Uncle Basile and I got started, we couldn't seem to stop at some walls and a roof, a couple of bedrooms, a living room, and a kitchen."

Diana saw movement from the corner of her eye, shrieked, and backed away so fast she almost tripped over the railing. "What is that?"

Raphael held out his arm, which had a small white snake wrapped around it. The small snake covered up most of Raphael's red and black snake tattoo. "It's a blue-eyed leucistic ball python. She's harmless, I promise."

Diana tried to get a better look without getting closer. She could see the snake's eyes were a very dark blue against the white skin. "I guess the tattoo isn't just for show."

"No, it's not for show. The snake my tattoo was based on was the one I had when I was young. She lived to be twenty-five. This one is a gift for my nephew. I've been getting her used to people. My sister is not thrilled with the idea, but Paul wants one. He's got good taste; this one here is a beauty."

Diana relaxed a little but was still unsure how close she wanted to get. The only snakes she'd seen were at the zoo. "I'll take your word for it. Does it have albinism?"

Raphael redirected the snake up his arm as it tried to slither off. "No. They're just white. A bit of a rarer breed, but I know people."

Diana took a step closer to get a better look. "What does it eat?"

Raphael didn't even hesitate. "Mice."

Diana's eyes shot up to his. She shuddered. "Well, don't ask me to feed her."

"Come on in, and I'll find something besides mice to feed you for breakfast."

Diana followed and was grateful when Raphael put the snake back in its tank. She hadn't noticed it on their tour yesterday. "You keep the snake in the kitchen?"

"Yes. But don't worry. Paul's birthday is in a few weeks."

"Yes, I know."

Diana could tell Raphael had forgotten for a moment who he was chatting with. "Right. I've got cereal, eggs, fruit, and toast."

Diana opted for fruit and toast, sorry that his friendly mood had vanished. It didn't take a genius to figure out he didn't like being reminded he was now married to the daughter of the man who had seduced and impregnated his teenage sister.

She had just finished breakfast when there was a honk outside. "That must be Adrian. He said he'd be here early."

Raphael picked up their breakfast dishes and set them

in the sink before following her outside.

Diana jogged to where Adrian was waiting. He was an earnest young man who lived with his elderly grandparents to help them out. "You're a lifesaver."

He shrugged his thin shoulders. "Any time. I have to get to work, so we'll need to empty this quickly."

Raphael came down the steps. The U-Haul was one of the smaller ones you towed with a car. "Didn't bring much, did you?"

She took the tote Adrian handed her. "As I said, I didn't see the point of bringing it all here."

Raphael and Adrian quickly unloaded her things onto the brick walkway. Diana carried one of the lighter boxes upstairs to her bedroom. They were done by the time she returned.

Diana pulled cash from her pocket and handed it to Adrian. "Thanks again, Adrian. Are you still good to return the trailer?"

"Yep, no prob. We got this unloaded quickly. You know where to find me if you need help moving anything else."

Raphael stood beside the totes, eyeing a large crate. "Nice kid. Is this thing heavy?"

Diana could scoot the crate, but not lift it. "I'll need help with it. The rest I can carry."

Raphael grunted but was able to get a good enough grip to lift it himself. It was heavy and bulky, but he managed to get it up the stairs to her room. "You sure you want all this in here?"

Diana simply nodded, only half listening. She went

about shoving the dresser to the other side of the room. "This will be perfect."

Raphael eyed the crate. "If you say so."

Diana protested when Raphael insisted on helping her carry the rest of her totes upstairs, but then relented. "Thank you. I'm going to unpack."

Raphael left.

Diana looked around the cluttered space. The clothes were easy enough. There was plenty of room in the walk-in closet and dresser to store her things. She hung her work clothes up next to her wedding suit. Next were her personal belongings She set picture frames with photos of her and her brothers, and Larissa and Shandy, on top of the dresser alongside her grandmother's jewelry box. That just left the tote she'd filled with everything from her bathroom. Since Raphael said the bathroom next door was hers, she dumped all her makeup and toiletries in there.

Finally, when all that was done, she tackled what she wanted to unpack the most. Even though she'd barely painted more than a few strokes these past months, it made her feel better to have her easel upright and her paints at hand. She dropped an oversized cloth covered in every color of paint imaginable on the floor to protect the wood and went about setting up her workspace. The light from the windows was perfect. The cheap folding cart on wheels was set in place beside her easel, and she packed it with her supplies. The canvases in the crate were all blank, so she just pushed the crate into the closet with her now empty totes. She preferred to stretch her own canvas, and instead of painting, she'd prepped enough canvases to keep her busy for months. She pulled one out and brought it to the easel and stared at the blank white fabric. If only she could find her inspiration again.

* * *

But as it had been for the past few months, her blank canvas was the least of her worries. She and Raphael managed to get through their first full day as man and wife without any major issues. Come Monday morning, she had much more on her mind than her husband. He had opted to take his car to Cabotage, and as soon as he arrived, he declared the office next to hers as his and firmly closed the door.

So where Diana had worried he'd be running her ragged, asking her dozens of questions, and consuming all her time, she'd barely seen him all morning. She could see her father's secretary, apparently Raphael's now, coming and going with files, various papers, and even a couple of cups of coffee.

Diana wasn't sure if that was a good sign or bad, but supposed it didn't matter one way or the other. She had enough on her plate. She'd been in touch with her attorney for tomorrow's competency hearing. She had been having Cabotage's legal team work on securing a few more contracts, while also dissolving a few. Her first order of business last week had been to cancel all orders in process for Gilbert Chamber's. She supposed she shouldn't have been surprised when she'd gotten a threatening letter from his attorney.

She was reading through the letter when Raphael strode into her office.

* * *

Raphael closed the door behind him without bothering to knock. "You've been running a tight ship these past months."

Diana set the letter down. "You sound surprised."

Raphael shrugged and took a seat. His eyes were tired from all the data he'd consumed that morning. He needed a break. For some reason, he had a desire to check in on his wife. And the fact that he was acknowledging her as a wife made him uneasy. But since he'd met Diana, she hadn't been far from his thoughts.

Raphael saw the letterhead printed at the top of the paper she'd set down. He spun it around. His jaw clenched as he read the letter. "When did you get this?"

Diana shrugged. "Came hand-delivered this morning."

"He has some nerve. I'll take care of this." Raphael well remembered how frightened Diana had looked, with her lip bleeding and her dress torn.

Diana plucked the letter from his fingers, her head down. "I'll take care of it. I know the last thing Cabotage needs is a lawsuit. But I was angry, and I canceled the orders and dictated a scathing letter. I shouldn't have canceled the orders. We are under contract until the end of the month."

Raphael could see her staring blankly at the wall, no doubt remembering when he'd threatened to beat

Chambers at the party. She probably had no intention of showing him that letter, but he'd caused the problem, and he'd fix it. "I said I'll take care of it. It's my problem now."

Diana dropped the letter in her desk drawer. "You don't own Cabotage yet. So until you do, I'm still in charge. We can't afford a lawsuit, nor can we fight him."

Raphael couldn't help the anger that burned in him. Nor the guilt. "I should have taken you to the police and had you press charges."

Diana rubbed her brow. "Wouldn't have done any good. And he's hardly the first."

Raphael felt the anger burn brighter. "What does that mean?"

Diana rose and turned her back on him. "He's hardly the first. My father's enemies are not exactly few. And there have been a few that tried to use me and my brothers against my father. So while Chamber's assault was frightening and a bit more aggressive than some, he's not the first. And now I've married one of his enemies. Not sure what that says about my intelligence."

Raphael crossed to her and turned her to face him. "I wouldn't hurt you."

Diana tipped her head and looked into his eyes. "Physically, perhaps not. But there are other types of hurt. When this is over, I've no doubt you'll hurt me, one way or another."

"And yet, believing that, you married me. I'm still trying to figure out why. I know the reasons you gave me, but I'm not convinced."

Diana's laugh lacked all humor. "A bit late for that, isn't

it?   We've made a deal.   We both have to live with it, whatever the outcome."

Raphael wanted to argue, but there was a knock at the door. "Your lapdog is at the door."

Diana glanced past Raphael to where Brett was waiting. "You'd do well to cultivate Brett's cooperation and loyalty. He's one of the few people who don't hate my father but would switch loyalties quickly. And he's not my lapdog."

Raphael opened the door. "Come on in."

Brett looked uncomfortable but came in. "I've got the contracts back from legal that you asked for. And you have a guest at the front desk."

Diana took them and flipped through them. "Who's at the front desk?"

"Benjamin Houghton."

Diana glanced up. "Ben's here?"

Raphael realized she didn't seem upset, angry, or any other emotion he might have expected when one of her father's enemies showed up looking for her. Ben Houghton had refused to sell his Cabotage shares to him, instead telling him he wanted to see how the takeover played out. The older man probably figured no matter which way he played it, he'd win in the end.   Raphael would pay handsomely to keep them out of Lanford's hands, and Lanford would have in turn offered more to keep them out of Raphael's hands. Assuming Lanford ever showed up.

Diana smiled. "Send him in, Brett. Thank you."

Raphael didn't budge from where he stood. And he decided to play dumb. "A friend of yours?"

"Yes. Ben is my godfather."

Now that did more than surprise Raphael.

Ben didn't bother to knock but opened the door. "Diana."

Diana gave him a huge smile. "Ben. I wasn't expecting to see you. It's been a while."

Ben let Diana cross to him. He hugged her and kissed her cheek. "Imagine my surprise when I heard the rumors this morning that you'd gotten married. And to Raphael Rouillard, of all people."

Diana held Ben for a moment before letting him go. "I wasn't sure how to tell you. And it was a bit sudden."

Ben turned and held a hand out to Raphael. He squeezed it hard when Raphael laid his hand in his. "After our chat last week, this was not what I thought you had in mind. What kind of game are you playing with little Di?"

"Little Di?"

"Don't play games with me, young man. I've devoured men and businesses more powerful than Rouillard. Last week you wanted my shares. Now you've married my goddaughter. I'm not feeling very friendly at the moment."

Diana took a step to bring her to Raphael's side. "There's absolutely nothing to worry about."

Ben's eyes narrowed, not convinced. "So you just happened to marry the man who's set on destroying everything your father worked for? A man who's using you for his own gain? One would think you'd have learned your lesson."

Diana paled. "This is not the same thing."

Ben swore. "I'm sorry, Diana. That was a low blow. But you aren't honestly going to stand here and tell me this is a love match."

Diana took Raphael's hand. "Perhaps not a love match. But a good match. I'd think you'd be happy to see me married."

"Not to a shark." Ben sighed. "All right, Diana. You don't look any worse for the wear, and you always were a smart girl. If you say it's a good match, then we'll leave it at that for now."

"Thank you, Ben."

Ben pointed his well-manicured finger at Raphael. "You step out of line or hurt her, you will regret it."

From a different man, Raphael might have ignored the threat. But he knew Benjamin Houghton's reputation. You didn't cross him, personally or in business, and not live to regret it. "My beef is with Lanford, not his daughter or his family."

"Good. So what exactly are you going to do?"

Raphael missed the warmth of Diana's hand as she left his side to go sit behind her desk. "Exactly what I said last week. I'm taking over Cabotage. And in the process, I'm releasing Diana from the burden of running it in her father's absence."

"Good. Diana might be an asset to Cabotage, but she belongs behind her canvases."

Diana laughed, this time with more than an ounce of humor. "Flatterer. You're still hoping to get your hands on the painting of your winery. It's my best work."

"I won't argue with you on that one. I still want it."

Diana opened her desk and pulled out a sheet of paper. "Take care of this, and I'll give it to you."

Raphael was still standing behind Ben. He saw Chamber's letterhead. "You shouldn't need a painting in return for that favor."

Ben read through the letter. "Diana, you canceled his orders. Why?"

Diana glanced at Raphael, but he couldn't read the expression on her face. "Let's just say he tried to use me to get back at Lanford. I didn't take too kindly to it."

Ben's fingers crushed the paper. "What exactly did he do?"

Raphael spoke up when it seemed that Diana had no intention of answering his question. "He assaulted her. Busted her lip and tore her dress. She wouldn't let me beat him to a pulp. So maybe siccing you on him will hit him where it hurts the most."

Raphael saw the immediate anger radiating from Ben. "I'll do better than beat him up. I'll destroy him. And I won't need a painting in return for that favor. It will be my pleasure."

Diana rose. "I just want that lawsuit to go away. I don't need a bunch of macho theatrics."

Ben folded the paper and tucked it into his pocket. "I'll take care of it."

"Thank you."

Ben took her hand across the desk. "Don't thank me yet. I had a secondary motive for coming. Where is your father, Diana? Raphael told me over the phone while trying to buy out my shares that Lanford has disappeared. Claims you're telling everyone he's out of the country. Your father is a fighter. He'd never stand on the sidelines while

Rouillard takes over his company."

"I don't know what else to tell you, Ben. He up and left. I've only heard from him a handful of times. I don't expect him back. I've got full control and autonomy over Cabotage in his absence; I even have the papers to prove it. Once the contracts are signed, Raphael will have control of Cabotage. The board already voted and agreed last week." She pointed to the papers Brett had handed her.

Raphael strode over and picked them up. He flipped through them. "This is the first time I've heard about a board vote."

Diana once again shrugged. "You owned more than half the shares two days after you filed papers with the SEC. Rouillard Enterprises has quite a reputation. Cabotage has been on shaky ground. The board believes you can revive the company. And our marriage succeeded in gaining the trust of several board members. This makes you the new president and CEO of Cabotage. Congratulations, Raphael; you win."

Ben took the contract from Raphael. He briefly read through it. "Well, well. If this doesn't get Lanford out of hiding, nothing will. You two have my blessing for now. Diana, I'll be over tomorrow for dinner."

Raphael was amused when Ben set the contract down and took Diana's hand and kissed her cheek again. "I guess we'll see you at dinner tomorrow. Where?"

Ben held his hand out. This time he didn't squeeze Raphael's hand, but simply shook it. "Diana's a great cook. You're in for a treat."

Diana picked the contract back up and held it out after

Ben left. "The quicker you sign this, the quicker you can claim control and boot my father out."

Raphael didn't take them. "Your godfather is a very powerful man. What did he mean when he said one would think you'd have learned your lesson?"

"I dated his youngest son. It didn't turn out well. I can't say Ben didn't warn me. But for a time, I thought Aiden and I made sense. But I was too young to understand what that meant. We dated for a while, and then we moved in together. We were together for four years. It wasn't until I was throwing him out that I realized how unbalanced our relationship was. Most men wanted to use me to get back at my father or to get close to him. I thought Aiden was different. And so he was. He wasn't interested in my father. But he was using me, nonetheless. It wasn't until his jealousy got toxic that I realized it. I thought we were in love, but it was the wrong kind. Any other questions?"

His first thought was to ask what kind of love it was. Beyond that, he had a dozen questions, but he couldn't ask, not with her trembling and her chin held high. He took the papers instead. This is why he married her, after all. He didn't like the feeling he was no different from all the other men in her life. But he couldn't pretend he didn't want something from her. And the more he was around her, the more he realized it wasn't just Cabotage he wanted.

Chapter Seven

Diana was humming to herself while she chopped vegetables and prepared dinner for Ben and Raphael. She enjoyed cooking for Ben. He always enjoyed the meals she prepared, and they had bonded over some of those meals.

Ben's wife had passed away when Diana was in her mid-twenties, while she'd been living with his son. After her passing, Ben spent a lot of time visiting his two sons. Ben's eldest son had taken over Ben's vineyard and had a very pretty wife and two beautiful children. Ben was happiest there. But he'd also wanted to spend more time with Aiden and Diana, in the hopes that a marriage would be in their future. Diana had not wanted Ben to know that her relationship with Aiden was tumbling around her. So she'd cooked family meals for the three of them and pretended everything was okay.

But Ben knew her as well as he did his son. And he knew something had been very wrong between them. But in his grief, for a time he'd ignored it. But it hadn't been long into one of their last family dinners that Ben encouraged her to break it off with Aiden. And after she had, she and Ben spent time together, each trying to heal from their respective losses.

She was also feeling extremely relieved now that the competency hearing had passed. The judge had granted her complete legal control of her father and his assets. And despite having disappeared for most of the day after insisting on driving herself into the office, Raphael had not asked any awkward questions. After the hearing, she'd stopped in to check on her father. He had been lucid when she'd gotten there, but it hadn't been long after she arrived that his mind started to drift once again. She slipped out when he'd closed his eyes and gone back to sleep. Hospice would start making visits now that she could make medical decisions for him, as he had been refusing their services. After she'd gotten off the phone with them, Diana had to fight back unwanted anger and grief as she struggled to come to grips with his slow decline.

But for now, things were settled again, and she could turn him over to professionals. And for Cabotage, she had Raphael's contract signed and locked away in her desk. She was grateful to be able to turn the business over to him, and some of the enormity of what she'd been dealing with had lightened.

Diana knew the moment Raphael came into the kitchen. She hadn't been in the office much that day, having claimed she needed to shop for the evening's meal. But she had been gone for hours, not returning to the office once she'd left. She had been unloading her car when Raphael pulled into the driveway with only two bags of groceries in her arms. He'd questioned her briefly, and she'd been purposefully vague about where she'd been all day.

Diana was humming off-key as he came to stand next to her. "That smells great."

Diana wiped her hands on the towel she'd left lying nearby. "Thank you. I forgot to ask you if you like seafood.

I hope dinner is satisfactory."

Raphael came to stand by the stove. "I'll eat almost anything. Lobster bisque?"

As Diana stirred the pot, she thought back to the meals they'd shared the last couple of days. Neither of them had much more than fruit, toast, and coffee in the morning. Sunday Raphael had grilled chicken and potatoes out on his patio, and then last night he'd made a stir fry using a package of precut chicken, frozen veggies, and rice. "Yes. And we're having salmon, wild rice, and sautéed vegetables in a light garlic sauce for the main course."

Raphael once again inhaled the scent. "I guess I should have put you in charge of the kitchen. My cooking is nowhere near on par with what you've got simmering in that pot. I suppose you'd have made dinner from scratch last night."

Diana next stirred the pot of wild rice and glanced over her shoulder at Raphael. "Probably. But I don't cook that much. Like most single people, I tend not to cook elaborate meals unless I have a good reason."

Raphael took some plates out of the cabinets and started to set the table. Food was another one of those things he didn't take for granted since getting out of prison, even though ten years had passed. His cooking wasn't fancy, but it was always plentiful.

Diana rummaged around. "Your kitchen is a little lacking. I can't find any serving dishes."

"I'm not big on dinner parties." Raphael nudged her out of the way and found a casserole pan that would have to do.

Diana turned to take the dish from him. Her mouth started to form the words "thank you," but her breath caught. He was only inches from her, and he was towering over her. But it wasn't fear that caused her hand to tremble for a moment. It certainly had not gotten past her notice that Raphael was an attractive man. As close as he was, she could see a darker ring of blue around his eyes. Her eyes dropped to his mouth, her sudden desire to have him kiss her taking her by surprise.

Raphael knew what she wanted, and he was tempted. And had she been anyone else, he would have taken her up on her offer. She had the sexiest mouth. But he was already having a hard enough time keeping his distance, remembering she was the enemy. So instead of acting on his impulses, he turned away from her and went back to setting the table.

Diana let out the breath she'd been holding. She'd seen the same desire in his eyes that she knew had been in hers. But then his eyes had gone cold, and he'd turned his back on her. Trying to regain her equilibrium, she went about assembling their meal. She found ceramic bowls to serve the bisque in and then set about combining the rice, vegetables, and salmon into the casserole dish. She was relieved when the doorbell rang, not wanting to face Raphael alone.

Raphael set down the cloth napkins he'd dug out of a drawer. "I'll get it."

Diana took a moment to compose herself before Raphael brought Ben to the kitchen.

"Hi." Diana met him halfway and kissed him on the

cheek.

Ben glanced around the large space. "I was telling Raphael that this is a great house. And the inside doesn't disappoint."

Diana agreed. "I instantly recognized it as a Basile Rouillard. I'm hoping I get a chance to meet him."

Ben gave her an odd look. "Given that you've married his nephew, one would have thought you would have met him already."

Raphael broke in to cover what he was sure would be an awkward excuse from Diana. "Uncle Basile has been on a cruise. He started seeing a woman a few months ago, and they've been inseparable. She convinced him to take a vacation."

Ben took a seat. "I know your uncle. I met him some years ago. He was the consummate bachelor back in those days."

"He claims now that he's getting older, he's ready to settle down. Her name is Rachel, and she's just a little younger than he is. He's been hinting at marriage. I guess we'll have to wait and see. But he's back at the end of this week and will be taking over my duties at Rouillard for the next couple of months while I get Cabotage back on its feet. He's looking forward to meeting Diana."

Satisfied with the answer, he thanked Diana as she set a bowl of bisque in front of him. "Join me, Raphael. As I said, you're in for a treat."

Raphael waited until Diana had brought two more bowls of bisque and the casserole dish. He held the chair out for her. She was surprised by the gesture, but he didn't notice.

Conversation during dinner mostly revolved around business. Ben had dozens of questions about Raphael's plans for Cabotage, more out of curiosity than any expectation that his shares were going to become more valuable.

After dessert, Ben turned down a second glass of wine and coffee. "Actually, Diana, I wanted to talk to you about your father's art collection. You didn't let the bank take it, did you?"

Diana stopped in her task of clearing the table. "You mean the Goodmans, don't you?"

Ben shrugged. "You know I've wanted to get my hands on those paintings for years. Your father bought them right out from under me."

Diana had heard the story. Ben had put money down to be the first to get a chance to buy the Goodman paintings that had come up for sale very unexpectedly. Assuming the paintings were authentic, they were worth a small fortune, and Ben had wanted them. She knew her father had come in and offered double whatever Ben had offered and had paid the man off to conveniently lose the signed agreement. Lanford ultimately bought the paintings for much more than they were worth.

Unfortunately, she didn't have them. If she did, she would sell them to Ben in a heartbeat. Just those three paintings alone would put her brothers through college. "I don't know what happened to them. They weren't on the yacht; I checked. The rest of the paintings I have in storage. I moved them myself. The only thing I can think of is that he sold them."

Ben's eyes narrowed as he contemplated his goddaughter. "A sale of that magnitude would have made waves. I've had a line on one of his last works for months, so I've been watching the market. You have to have them. Where else would he have hidden them?"

Diana was surprised by Ben's forceful tone, but she supposed that given the relationship he had with her father, it was to be expected. Stabbing friends in the back was one of Lanford's specialties. "I don't know. I've been through his papers, both at home and at the office. I didn't see any mention of them being sold. But he isn't always one to do things by the book. I don't know if he has any other safety deposit boxes or anything stored in a bank vault. But if I find them, I'll let you know."

Ben rose to help clean the table. "Your father always was a wily one. And you're right, he isn't one to do things by the book. But if you find them, I'll pay you handsomely for them."

Diana nodded and took the dishes from his hand. "I'll take care of this. Have Raphael show you his collection. He has a Brockman. It's beautiful. He also has a painting by the mystery artist, D.E."

Raphael responded. "Diana was quite taken with it when she arrived. She was more interested in my paintings than moving in. If she ever decides to leave, I may have to put it under lock and key."

Ben laughed. "I'm guessing that after dinner tonight you've found another reason to give her plenty of reasons to stay."

Raphael nodded at that, his eyes on Diana as he spoke to Ben. "The meal was amazing. You didn't oversell it."

Diana wasn't one to blush, but she felt heat rising to her cheeks. "When you're done looking at the art, you can see his snake."

Raphael gestured toward his office. "I'll show you my extremely limited collection. I'm guessing your collection wouldn't fit in an office."

Diana let out a soft breath as the men left the room. Perhaps sending the men off alone wasn't a great plan, but she needed a moment to regain her equilibrium and get her emotions back under control.

* * *

Raphael led Ben to his office, but his thoughts lingered on Diana as he led the way. It had been an odd couple of days. Though he'd participated in the conversation at dinner, his mind kept drifting back to their meeting yesterday.

Despite an odd moment of hesitation he couldn't understand, he'd signed the contracts right after Ben left that now put him solely in charge of Cabotage. Once that had been taken care of, he'd not had much time to worry about his hesitation, or about what Diana had been up to today while he'd been up to his eyebrows in contracts and phone calls. He couldn't afford to spend much time away from Rouillard Enterprises, so his first order of business was to leave a message for his uncle that things had gone as planned, and that he looked forward to his return next week. Raphael needed him to manage the reins at Rouillard while he sorted out the mess Lanford had left when he'd disappeared. He already had a man in mind to manage Cabotage once he'd reestablished the business.

Ben followed Raphael. Front and center was Diana's painting. "You have good taste. And a good eye. I'd hold onto this one if I were you. It's going to be worth more than the Goodmans one day."

Raphael eyed the painting, not seeing what he was sure both Diana and Ben saw when they looked at it. "I'm not familiar with Goodman."

"Harlan Goodman was the son of a Texas oil baron. More money than you, me, and Lanford put together. He was quite spoiled, having been raised mostly by his mother. She indulged him, and painting became the only thing Harlan cared about. His father wasn't thrilled. He wanted his son to take over his holdings. But it became clear quite quickly that he didn't have his father's talent. He did have a daughter who did. She inherited the entire corporation. Harlan shrugged it off, as only someone incredibly arrogant or incredibly ignorant could do. Thankfully for him, his mother set money aside for him before his father died. But he quickly squandered it and ended up living off the charity of his sister."

"I take it he wasn't famous during his lifetime."

"Sadly, no. He had quite the reputation with the ladies, though. He was murdered by a jealous lover. She burned all of his art that was in his possession when he died. And of course, the scarcity of his work made the ones collectors held that much more valuable. And like with most things one can collect, what was out there started going to the highest bidder. But I had a personal reason for wanting the Goodman paintings that Lanford bought."

Raphael eyed the older man when he dropped silent. "What was the personal reason?"

Ben blinked and focused back on Raphael. "The model in the three paintings was my mother. Goodman was my father. She hadn't told him she was pregnant before he died. And his family wasn't interested in Harlan Goodman's bastard son. But my mother did convince his sister to contribute to my financial well-being. Years after I was born, it became apparent I had inherited my grandfather's business acumen. The first company I took over belonged to my grandfather, even though his daughter was managing it. He was ninety at the time."

Raphael knew the stories of Benjamin Houghton's many hostile takeovers. When Ben had called him a shark, it was a case of it takes one to know one. "That's some story. Diana knows?"

Ben glanced back into the kitchen where Diana was washing dishes. "She knows. Most people do. Unfortunately, Lanford knew, too. He knew I'd pay almost anything for those paintings of my mother. He was furious when I refused to pay his asking price."

Given what Raphael knew of the man, he couldn't help but speculate. "You don't suppose he destroyed them, do you?"

"No. He was always a patient man. He'd remind me from time to time that he had them. And that the price went up every year I didn't buy them from him. If you hadn't taken over his company, I would have. He would have given me anything to get his company back."

"Until he disappeared. No one seems to know where he is except Diana."

Ben nodded. "I haven't been able to find him, not that I've been looking. I was going to hire a discreet investigator to look into his sudden disappearance, but when you filed intent with the SEC, I decided to let this play out your way. I figure between you and the bank, the paintings will surface. But if Diana's telling the truth and she doesn't know where they are, then she could be in danger."

That got Raphael's immediate interest. "Danger? What kind of danger?"

Ben crossed the room and took a seat on the dark brown leather sofa. "Collectors are often eccentric, but not often dangerous. But those paintings are considered priceless by some, and I know a few dangerous men who would love to get their hands on them. I saw the bank inventory of what they took possession of. And there was not a single painting on that list. I know Diana well enough to know she would have taken those paintings. I don't know where Lanford is, but I promise you he has assets stashed. And when he resurfaces, assuming the bank did get a hold of them and he doesn't know where they are, he'll just be one of many looking to cash in on those Goodmans when they turn up."

"So if Lanford has had them all these years, and if these men are dangerous, why didn't they just do away with him and take them?"

Ben contemplated a painting across from his place on

the couch. "Lanford knows a lot of secrets. Secrets people will pay to keep quiet. Some would argue Lanford should have been disposed of years ago. But Lanford claims to have evidence against certain people, and should anything happen to him, that evidence would be made public. These men believe that threat, and in turn, see to his continued good health and welfare."

Raphael thought about the man who confronted Diana about her father's whereabouts. "But his disappearance must have a lot of those men nervous. Men who might try to use Diana to find out where he is."

Satisfied that Raphael understood where he was going with this conversation, Ben rose. "Exactly. Diana doesn't know her father made most of his money in blackmail. She has always believed his business was the source of his money. The business has done well over the years, but it doesn't account for all that he had amassed. Unless Lanford turns up, I fear what might happen if these men get anxious and try to use Diana to flush him out. Now that the bank has taken all his assets and since he's been missing, these men may no longer believe he has the evidence against them. They may simply want him to permanently disappear. And if that's the case, they'll use any means necessary."

Raphael cursed. "Including Diana. She's been all over the press and has been written up in every newspaper and business magazine since taking the helm of Cabotage. Her answers as to where he is have been vague. All she'll say is that he's out of the country. There is a ton of speculation as to where Lanford might be hiding."

"Take care of her, Raphael. I have a feeling you're the perfect man for the job. You might be one of the only men Lanford hasn't been able to manipulate over the years."

Raphael's jaw clenched. "I'd say getting me tossed in jail was a win on his part."

Ben simply shook his head. "He was afraid of you. He didn't have secrets he could lord over you. Your time in jail was a brief reprieve at best. I don't know if he knows you married his daughter yet, but you hold a pretty powerful weapon in your hands right now. Through Diana and the secrets she doesn't know she holds, you could destroy him."

"And that's what you're hoping, isn't it?"

Ben didn't reply. He looked over at Diana through the open office door. "As I said, you have good taste. You need to be the one to flush Lanford out, for your wife's sake if no one else's. When he shows up, the target will be off her back and on his. From there, all you have to do is let nature take its course."

Raphael left the office, Ben trailing behind him. He watched as Diana finished up the dishes. Did she know where her father was? Did she know the secrets he kept? Before he had married her, he would have believed she did. But the more he got to know Diana, the more he couldn't believe it. She was smart. There was no doubt of that. She loved her brothers. There was no doubt of that either. She was capable of consorting with her father in his blackmail schemes. But Raphael couldn't get it to play out in his mind. He believed she was innocent in this; another pawn in the games her father played.

* * *

Diana turned to see Raphael and Ben behind her. She gave them a small smile. "What do you think?"

Ben kissed her cheek. "I think he has great taste. I should go. I have an appointment with some investors in the morning about an expansion of the winery."

"You know, when people retire, they don't keep expanding their empires."

Ben chuckled as he grabbed the suit jacket he'd discarded earlier. "Just one of the many reasons I let Raphael here take over Cabotage. A few years ago, he'd have had a fight on his hands if the circumstances had been the same."

Diana walked Ben to the door. "Things might have been better if you had fought Lanford harder."

Ben just shook his head. "Things are as they are meant to be. Take care of yourself, Diana. And don't trust anyone other than Raphael."

"You know how ridiculous that sounds, don't you? Raphael is probably the last man I should trust."

Ben looked past her to where Raphael was, his eyes seeking out the younger man's. "You married him, so there must be some trust there. In business, I wouldn't trust him. But personally, you could do worse."

She had done much worse, in her opinion, but Diana kept that to herself. While her relationship with Aiden was a long time ago, he was still Benjamin's son. She made it a point to keep her opinion that his son was the worst to herself. "See you, Ben."

* * *

Ben waved and headed for his car. He truly cared for Diana and didn't want to see her hurt. He only hoped Raphael took his words seriously. The dominoes that were aligned were about to fall.

Chapter Eight

For the rest of the week, Raphael was so busy with Cabotage that it wasn't hard for Diana to leave the office and be back before he knew she was gone. The morning after their dinner with Ben, she'd had an appointment with the funeral home to finalize the arrangements for her father's passing. Other than her brothers, she couldn't imagine anyone else wanting to come to a memorial service. Larissa would come, if for no other reason than to be beside her sons. It was likely Shandy would make the trip for the same reason. She opted for a brief wake, a small viewing for family only, and subsequent cremation. She doubted anyone would want his ashes, so she arranged for them to be interred at a nearby cemetery with a small plaque.

But mostly she was glad Raphael was busy so she could stop by her condo and see how her father was, without his questioning where she was going. Most days she took her car to the office so she could leave at will. This morning's visit had been particularly difficult because her father was more lucid than he'd been during her last few visits. He was furious about being at her condo, furious that he was stuck in a bed, and generally furious that for the first time in his life, he wasn't in control.

It hadn't gotten past her notice that he hadn't been furious that no one was visiting him. He didn't ask about his sons or his wife. Most of his questions were about money or Cabotage. She told him as little as possible. She hadn't told him he no longer had control of his affairs; that she now controlled his life. She hadn't told him that Raphael now had control of his company. He seemed to have forgotten the day she'd gone to Raphael's office, and she hadn't bothered to remind him. The doctor had warned her that his short-term memory was being affected by the tumor, and in some ways, she saw that as a blessing.

Watching him deteriorate, she couldn't stop the stirring of pity she felt as he lay in the hospital bed. She had imagined throwing the fact that he was under her control in his face. She had imagined how satisfying it would feel to tell him Cabotage was now under Raphael's control. But as pity and guilt churned in her stomach, she found herself simply reassuring him that she was firmly in control of the company and not to worry.

One thing her father didn't deserve was pity. He'd spent his whole life isolating himself from the people who wanted to love him. And because of that, the best place for him was tucked away at her condo until he breathed his last breath. But guilt did eat at her. She still hadn't painted; she had lost a couple more pounds, and the burden she was carrying weighed heavily on her. She was the only one in the family who knew he was ill. And seeing his mind and body deteriorate more and more, she knew it was time to tell the family. There was just one last thing to do first.

"You've been staring off into space for a few minutes. Everything all right?"

Diana started at the sound of Brett's voice. "Sorry. I've had a lot on my mind lately. Need something?"

"No. Just checking in. Mr. Rouillard seems to be busy and doesn't want to be disturbed. And I guess I'm surprised you keep coming in. I expected you to bail."

"Soon. I hope. But I want everyone to feel more secure about the merger before I permanently hang up my suit jacket."

Raphael didn't knock when he opened the door. "Conspiring in here?"

Diana smiled at him, too tired to take offense. "Not today. Brett was just saying you were not to be disturbed."

Raphael looked at Brett, who took the hint and left. "He's good at his job. I see why your father hired him. But I think his loyalty lies with you, not your father."

Diana shrugged. "Possibly. Working in operations, Brett has a close relationship with the people at the plant. I think it's more his allegiance to them that has kept him here all these years. And my father, for all his many faults, pays his staff well. So what brings you here?"

"Today's the big day, right? Your brothers will officially be college students."

Diana glanced at the clock. She still had a few minutes, but she was going with her brothers to sign up for classes. She'd paid the deposit, so they had dorm rooms reserved for the school year. And though they were more than capable, she wanted to be there. And since she'd paid a good chunk of their tuition already, they were feeling indulgent enough to allow her to come.

"Yes. It's so hard to believe that in a few months they'll officially be attending university full-time."

Raphael leaned against the wall. "You and Larissa did a

good job raising them."

"I can't take much credit. I was pretty wrapped up in my own life for a while. But I like to think I was a good influence, anyway. Someone besides their mother whom they could look up to."

"Any word from your father yet?"

She knew Raphael had been sure once it became public knowledge he was now in charge of Cabotage that Lanford would come out of hiding. No doubt he was as surprised as everyone else that there had been no word from him yet. And Diana couldn't help but wonder if Raphael would now hire an investigator to find him. And she feared what an investigator would uncover. Diana started packing up her bag so she wouldn't have to look him in the eye when she lied. "Not yet."

"Would you tell me?" Raphael crossed the room and planted his hands on the desk. "You've been hiding something; don't think I haven't noticed."

"You're being paranoid."

Raphael leaned closer. "I don't think so. But we can talk about it later."

Diana snatched up her purse and tried to be calm as she exited the office. It was so tempting to lean on Raphael. To tell him the truth and let the chips fall where they may. But the longer she held her secrets, the harder they became to tell.

* * *

Diana followed behind her brothers as they talked

excitedly about the classes they'd signed up for. Since their interests and majors were the same, they had signed up for as many classes together as had been available. As far as she could tell, the only class they wouldn't share was speech.

Diana had felt a bit nostalgic as she'd walked the campus with her brothers, though she had gone to an art college in New York City. College seemed so many years ago. There were times when she stood next to her brothers that she felt much older than her thirty-two years. Part of her wanted to congratulate them and take off. The other part knew it was past time she told them the truth.

Nick dropped back a couple of steps and wrapped his arms around Diana's waist so they were walking side by side. "Let's eat. I'm starving. And I think Diana should buy, now that we're poor college students."

Diana raised a brow but didn't bother to point out that she'd just paid for their dorm and first year's tuition. "Let me guess. Pizza."

Drew turned and walked backward so he could see Diana and Nick. "How did you know?"

Diana bumped her hip against Nick. "Lucky guess."

They hit up the campus bookstore first and lugged the purchases back to the car. Diana drove them to their favorite pizza place. The boys ordered a large with everything on it. Diana pointed to a table outside, away from the crowd.

Diana waited until they finished their pizza. "We need to talk."

Nick gulped down the last of his soda. "Such a serious face."

Diana spun her still full plate. "I forget how grown you two are sometimes. I'm so proud of both of you. You know that, don't you?"

"Jeez, Di." Drew turned slightly pink.

"Sorry. There's something I need to tell you. I wanted you to finish high school, and I needed to take care of some things first."

Diana told her brothers how their father had been diagnosed with cancer, and how it had spread quickly. She told them about his stroke and memory loss. She told them how she needed to secure the company, sell her shares, and get power of attorney before she told anyone.

She thought they took it well. They were angry at first that she hadn't told them; that she had been lying. Struggling not to cry, she explained that his illness needed to remain a secret just a little longer, at least until Raphael had secured his position at the company and the business was settled. Too many people relied on Cabotage. Then she told them Raphael didn't know about the illness, and that it was better he didn't.

She then drove them to her condo so they could see for themselves. Drew, the more compassionate of the two, had shed some tears over his father's deteriorated state. Nick, who was much less forgiving, had simply stared at his father. Both of them promised to keep it from Raphael but weren't going to keep it from their mother.

For Diana, she was just glad Lanford remained asleep during the visit. She had left the two young men with their father while she went to chat with the nurse.

Diana wasn't surprised when the nurse told her she was

sure Lanford had another small stroke. It would only be a matter of weeks at this point, possibly even days. Diana wouldn't be surprised if Lanford held on a little longer, just out of spite. She knew it was a risk to tell her brothers, and in turn, Larissa. The rest of the paperwork had been filed; she just needed a little more time for her lawyer to finish the contracts to sell Raphael Lanford's shares. At that point, Diana supposed it wouldn't matter if the truth came out, though she'd rather it stay hidden until Lanford's passing and after she hopped on a plane.

Diana was sitting on her sofa in her living room when the doorbell rang. She rose and pulled open the door, knowing it would be Larissa on the other side.

Larissa swallowed the lump in her throat and glanced past Diana. "Nick called and told me about Lanford. I can't believe you've been keeping this a secret."

Diana softly closed the door as Larissa came into the living area. She could tell Larissa was feeling much as she was. A combination of guilt and hatred. "The boys had a similar reaction. I'll tell you what I told them. I didn't have a choice. There is too much at stake."

Larissa sat on the couch, dropping her head in her hands instead of heading to the bedroom where she could hear the soft voices of her sons. "I thought about that on the way over. Your marriage to Raphael makes sense now. But I'm still unsure what role he's playing in this."

Diana took a seat at the other end of the sofa. "Raphael agreed to buy Lanford's shares at twenty percent over their face value before our marriage, once they're in my possession. That money will pay most of the boys' tuition.

Truth is, I funded the dorm rooms and the first year's tuition from my savings and with a loan. I didn't tell Nick and Drew that, and I'd appreciate it if you didn't either. I've been trying to juggle the business; trying to figure out how to keep it afloat. Raphael's timing of the takeover ended up being beneficial for both of us."

Larissa rubbed her forehead, trying to lessen the brewing headache. "Lanford was always great at keeping secrets. If we were talking about anything other than Cabotage, he'd probably applaud you."

"The thought has occurred to me." Diana scooted over so she could take Larissa's hand. "It won't be much longer. A couple of weeks at most. You're welcome to come as often as you'd like."

Larissa shook her head. "I won't bother to pretend affection. We stayed married for the children. Our relationship has been over for years. He's barely been around the past two. His mistresses saw him more than I did. Drew and Nick saw him even less. I haven't thanked you for seeing to the house when the bank foreclosed. Or for the boys. I can't afford to put them through college. So thank you for that. Truly. I don't know how we're going to manage a funeral. But I suppose I need to deal with it when the time comes."

Diana let Larissa's hand go and rose. "Arrangements have been taken care of. I didn't think you'd mind."

Larissa trembled, but only felt relief. "Thank you, Diana. I don't know if I could have handled it. It wasn't always like this, you know. Once upon a time, I did love him."

"I know. And I was grateful when you married him. And when you had Drew and Nick. But I could see how much he hurt you. How he hurt all of us."

Larissa wiped at the lone tear that squeezed past her lashes. "He was always a workaholic. That never bothered me. My dad was, too, so it seemed normal to me. But my dad never cheated on my mom. The first time Lanford cheated, I was devastated. By the third or fourth time, it became the norm. I had Nick and Drew to worry about, and I was so afraid to be on my own. I thought about divorce, but it just seemed easier to stay married. That's my shame to bear; that I stayed out of comfort. And it's even odder now that I know he's dying. I'm not sad, not really. He abandoned us two years ago. There is nothing left; no house, no money. The bank took everything. And I just can't care."

"I kept the artwork. Half belongs to you. I can help you sell it. You won't have nothing when this is over. It won't be enough to pay for Nick's and Drew's schooling, and it won't buy you a condo. But it might be enough for a down payment and will help keep a roof over your head for a while."

Larissa brushed away a second tear and rose. She hugged Diana. "I wish you were my daughter, Diana. Perhaps I wouldn't feel so guilty accepting half. It will be enough to get me to Philadelphia and time to figure out the next step in my life. And I'll be forever grateful to you for what you've done for Nick and Drew."

Diana let Larissa lean on her for a moment, understanding her stepmother's mixed emotions. She kept the older woman's hand in hers as she took her to the bedroom and left her with her sons and husband.

It was a couple more hours before the trio left. Diana had hugged her brothers and stepmother again before they left. She spoke with the nurse one last time before leaving. Diana struggled against more tears as she drove back to Raphael's.

It was well past dinner before she closed the front door behind her. She heard rock music coming from the kitchen, so she knew where he was. She was tempted to go to her room and hide but found herself heading his way. She didn't shudder as she passed the tank with the snake in it. She found herself getting used to the creature, so long as it was locked up in the tank.

Raphael tossed some spices into the pot he was stirring but knew the moment Diana entered the kitchen. "I wasn't sure when you'd be back. And I bet the boys made you feed them."

Diana found her lips curling at his comment. He'd only met them once but seemed to know them better than their father did. "Pizza. That smells wonderful."

Raphael stirred the pot a few more times before putting the lid on. "More Italian, I'm afraid. I had an urge for spaghetti."

Diana set her purse on the counter and took a couple of plates out of the cupboard. "I didn't eat much of the pizza. They ordered the works, and I do mean the works. I just can't bring myself to eat anchovies on a pizza."

Raphael glanced over at Diana. "In prison, you're hungry enough to eat whatever they put in front of you. I'd have killed for a pizza, even with anchovies."

Diana put a hand to the spot burning in her gut. "I'm sorry."

Raphael shrugged and grabbed a pair of forks. "Nothing to be sorry for. Just a fact."

Diana set a hand on his forearm. "Doesn't make me not sorry."

Raphael was about to pull his arm away when he looked into her eyes. The sadness that was ever-present in her topaz eyes was particularly strong tonight. "Rough day?"

She cast her eyes down to where her hand rested on his arm. "It was harder than I thought; that's all."

Raphael used the back of his fingers to lift her chin. "This isn't about your brothers. I meant it earlier when I said we need to talk. I don't like secrets or lies. Big enough ones can even land you in prison."

Diana thought of Adeline and her secret relationship with Lanford and the lies that Lanford told that ultimately landed Raphael in prison. "I promise my secrets will never hurt you. And they won't land anyone in prison."

Raphael's eyes narrowed. "So you admit you have them."

Diana slid her hand down Raphael's arm to his wrist, covering the snake tattoo with her fingers. "Just one. It might make you really mad, but it won't hurt you. It won't hurt anyone. Not even me."

Diana's fingers circled Raphael's wrist, her fingers on his pulse. His fingers went from her chin to her cheek. Raphael bent his head to hers. His mouth was just a breath from hers. "Diana?"

Knowing it was probably a mistake, her grip tightened on his wrist. "Yes."

Diana opened her mouth under the demands of his kiss. Somehow, she knew he'd be forceful in this as he was in other parts of his life. Not caring that he didn't even like her, she found her fingers gripping his hair, her hips pressing into his, her mouth open under his, welcoming the forceful kiss.

She reveled in the kiss when Raphael pulled her hips closer, and his tongue delved into her mouth. The taste of him was heady, her breasts were crushed against his chest, and she could feel the painful grip of his fingers in her hair. As tempting as it was to let him finish what he'd started, she found herself pulling back when he tried to bring her even closer. She felt a moment of regret when his grip loosened and he used his hands to steady her instead of pulling her closer. He held her so that she was still trapped between him and the counter, but their bodies were no longer touching.

Diana opened her eyes, her fingers loosening in his hair. His eyes were a stormy blue this time, his breath as quick as hers. She wasn't sure what to say, if anything. She'd enjoyed that kiss more than any other man's before. She could feel her body tightening in anticipation of more to come. But the hard look in his eyes, though not angry or disgusted, had her scooting out of reach.

Raphael watched Diana as she picked up the plates she'd set down on the counter and took them to the table. Shaking off the kiss and his odd mood, he turned back to the stove. The water in the other pot was boiling. He tossed in the pasta.

The pair was silent as they finished preparing dinner. Diana mostly just stayed out of Raphael's way. She also kept quiet until he fixed her a plate with enough food for two people on it.

"I can't eat all that." Diana eyed the plate.

"As far as I can tell, you barely eat at all. You're going to waste away at the rate you're going. Whatever secret you have, it's eating you up from the inside out."

Diana picked up the fork and swirled a small bite. She closed her eyes at the wonderful flavor of the sauce. "I think you've found your calling."

Raphael wanted to push her until she opened up to him, but her enjoyment of the meal stopped him. "It's my great-grandmother's recipe."

She forked up another bite. "If you ever decide to get out of the rat race, you could open a restaurant and serve nothing but this spaghetti."

Amused, he took a large bite. "This was the first thing I made when I got out of prison. I stayed with my uncle. Adeline was a bit put out with me for it. She wanted me to stay with her. But she had Paul to worry about; I didn't want her worrying over me any more than she already was."

Diana stopped with the fork halfway to her mouth. "Does she blame herself for what happened?"

Raphael finished his bite before answering, chewing longer than necessary to postpone answering the question. With a deep sigh, he nodded. "She spent the entire time I was in prison doing everything in her power to try to get me out. Between Paul, work, and her worrying about me, she was on the brink of collapse. Every time she visited me in prison, I could see the guilt of it eating away at her. It was like that for the first year. I was so grateful when she met Kevin. He could see what stress and worry were doing to her. He was the one who finally convinced her it wasn't her fault."

Diana could picture Adeline as she had been that day in the courtroom. "I imagine it took some persistence on his part."

"He can be as stubborn as she is. But it was my choice that landed me in jail, with the help of Lanford and his money. I knew what type of man he was, but I thought I had right on my side. I was wrong."

Diana could hear the anger in his words. "He's always been that way. He never cared who he had to step over or step on to get his way. He was afraid of you. I would bet you're one of the few people who ever really scared him."

"Your father's reaction is and always has been to fight. So where is he, Diana? He's not the type to let his company go without a fight. Is he dead?"

Diana felt herself pale. "Dead?"

Raphael stabbed his fork into his dinner. "I figure nothing short of death would keep him away."

Diana slowly shook her head, the movement barely perceptible. "No, he's not dead. But he doesn't know about the company."

"Then how do you suppose you're going to talk him into selling his shares if he doesn't know the company is no longer under his control?"

Diana set her fork down. "You've never believed I would get those shares, anyway. So why do you care?"

"I don't like games, Diana."

She looked at his mouth. "Then what was that kiss?"

His hand shot out and took her hand. "No game. I want you."

Her hand trembled under his. With her other hand, she traced the snake's head on his wrist. "I think you might be out of my league."

His fingers tightened on her hand. "Don't you mean that the other way around? You're too good for an ex-con. You're too classy, too refined, for the likes of me. Too good for a man with violence in him."

Diana tugged her hand free. "There was a time in my youth I would have thought those things. But I meant what I said. I've no doubt you're a dangerous man, Raphael. But despite our past histories, you've been kind to me. You would have beaten Chambers on my behalf for what he tried to do to me, and he'd have deserved it. But you didn't because I asked you not to. Your sister adores you, and despite your past and being older than her, she'd do anything to protect you. Kevin came out in the middle of the night to help you because you asked. You inspire loyalty. Those are good qualities, Raphael. I don't deserve them."

Diana rose and made it halfway out of the room before she turned around. "I'm not afraid of you. Maybe I'm afraid of myself. I wish I had your strength in me. But I'm too soft, and I don't know how to fight for what I want. So I'll keep my secrets until I'm ready to reveal them. You can either accept that or ask me to leave. Your choice."

* * *

Raphael didn't try to stop her as she went upstairs, though his mind was still on their kiss. He'd thought about kissing her more times than he cared to admit. He spent a lot of his time thinking about her long legs, the way her blouses molded her breasts, and how much he'd like to touch and taste. By all rights, she was his enemy, but when she'd shifted to get closer to him, rising on her toes to increase the pressure of the kiss, it was hard to remember that fact. And now that he'd kissed her, he couldn't wait to do it again.

Instead of following her, he finished his meal, taking her plate and wrapping it for later. She'd eaten more than he'd thought she would, a testament to her enjoyment of it, but had not eaten nearly enough. He tried to be annoyed by the protective instincts she aroused in him but couldn't muster any. He wanted to wrap her in his arms and promise to fight her battles for her. To promise to help carry those secrets.

But she was right about one thing. She was too soft. Not physically, but emotionally. And he was the type of man who inevitably bruised soft feelings. His sister and his ex-fiancée could attest to that.

Chapter Nine

Raphael punched the large bag Kevin held. Once or twice a week, the two men would hit the local gym. Raphael spent so much time behind a desk that he needed a physical outlet. He got up early each morning, long before Diana came downstairs, and worked out his frustrations in his home gym in his basement. But it was nice to spend an evening or two with Kevin. They'd even started bringing Paul now that he was getting older. But tonight he was at home hanging out with friends.

Kevin grunted at the impact of Raphael's fist against the bag. "Women trouble?"

Raphael grunted back. "I don't have a woman."

"Diana sure looks like a woman to me."

Raphael gave the bag one last solid punch. "She's not mine."

Kevin released the bag. "You married her. I'd say you have a pretty solid claim of ownership there."

Raphael blotted the sweat from his forehead. "Adeline would smack you for saying that."

"Nah, she likes it. And turnabout is fair play. I am definitely hers."

Raphael picked up his bottle of water and took a large swallow. "And it better stay that way."

Kevin held up both hands as he headed to the treadmill. "No worries there. So, what's up? Diana causing you trouble?"

Raphael joined him. "Not trouble exactly. She's keeping secrets and doesn't deny it. Says I can accept them or kick her out."

Kevin kicked up the speed. "I take it you're accepting them. Somehow, I can't see you kicking her out."

"That's what bothers me. She's nothing to me. I got what I wanted from her while keeping my promise to Adeline. It was Diana's idea to move in with me while we are married, though I would have insisted if she hadn't. But if I had any sense, I'd ask her to leave."

"You like her, don't you? I didn't know you before prison, but you don't give the women you meet your full attention. I'd say Diana is the first woman in the years I've known you that you've shown real interest in, outside of a one-night stand or a short-term arrangement."

Raphael didn't like how close to home that comment hit. He could think of no other woman he thought about as much as he did Diana, before or after prison. He'd been engaged before going to prison. His fiancée hadn't stuck around longer than it took to clear out their apartment and his bank account after he'd been arrested. She was gone before he was released on bail, and he hadn't bothered to go look for her. So much for the love she claimed to have for him.

After he'd gotten out of jail, he hadn't had what one would call a committed relationship. There were plenty of women out there willing to spend a night or two with him. But he hadn't been interested in anything beyond that.

Diana was different from those women. He was

different around her. When she was relaxed, he enjoyed her company. He liked sharing dinner and a conversation with her. He didn't only think about sex when he was around her, though he'd thought about it plenty, especially since that kiss. He had the urge to fix all her problems, to promise her he'd be there for her, unlike her father, who never committed to anyone or anything other than Cabotage.

The truth was he liked Diana Kennedy. A lot. Given time, he could see their marriage become the real thing. He wasn't sure how she felt about it. But there had been enough heat in their kiss to know she desired him. It was a place to start. And he remembered well when she'd told Ben they were a good match, and he wondered if she meant it. The more he was around her, the more he agreed. Socially they meshed. They knew many of the same people and moved in the same circles since she had come back to Cabotage. She understood his work, which would make things easier when he worked late or had work on his mind and didn't give her much attention. He was sure he had more money than she did, but she had plenty of her own. The time they spent together was comfortable. She didn't seem to mind it when he was quiet, nor did he feel like he had to entertain her. For him, a man who hadn't had many committed relationships, she seemed to blend into his life seamlessly. As long as he didn't focus on her secrets.

The two men ran for a while, then did a cool-down walk. When they reached the locker room, Kevin spoke, concern lacing his voice. "Paul's been asking about her."

Raphael was jerked back to reality from his wandering

thoughts. "What does Adeline say?"

"She's not sure. She doesn't want to keep Paul from knowing Diana and her brothers, necessarily. But Diana means Lanford, and Adeline gets fiercely protective when it comes to keeping Lanford away from her son."

Raphael stripped off his sweaty t-shirt. "Lanford has no interest in him. He has two other sons and a wife he ignores. If it weren't for the fact that he seems to need Diana to run Cabotage in his absence, I doubt he would pay her much attention either."

Kevin grabbed his bag, intending to shower at home. "Adeline wants to invite you both over for dinner. I told her to wait a little longer. Let things between the two of you settle."

Raphael grimaced. "I don't know how long that will take."

Kevin slung his bag over his shoulder. "I saw the way you looked at her the night we drove her home. Your protective instincts were in high gear that night. And if I'm not mistaken, so was your libido."

He hated that he was so transparent. Diana wasn't the only one good at keeping secrets, and he preferred to keep his feelings on tight reins. "Go home to your wife. And I agree, tell Adeline to wait a little while before inviting us over. Until I know what she's hiding, I'd like to keep Adeline and Paul away from her."

Kevin could only agree. He loved Paul the same as if he were his blood, and he wouldn't let anyone hurt him. "All right. Night."

Raphael hit the showers before driving home. It gave

him a little more time to think. He had been avoiding Diana for the past couple of days, trying to sort through what he was feeling. And if he weren't mistaken, she was avoiding him as well. He only hoped her thoughts were in the same vein as his.

He was halfway home when his phone rang. He frowned when he saw it was Diana. "I'm almost home."

Diana's voice was soft. "I'm at Cabotage. My office has been ransacked. I called the police, and they've come and gone."

Raphael flipped on his turn signal and made a quick turn, heading in the opposite direction. "Just your office?"

"Yes."

"On my way." Raphael hung up the call and made his way quickly through the light evening traffic.

A security guard was at the front desk, looking upset. Raphael glanced at him, his expression fierce. The guard didn't make eye contact. He'd deal with him later. No one was supposed to be coming or going at this hour of the night. Raphael ignored the elevator in favor of the stairs, taking the three flights in double steps.

The office was quiet. Another security guard was standing by the entryway. Raphael gave the man a sharp look, who in turn used his security badge to open the door for him. When he got to Diana's office door, he stopped in his tracks. Framed photos were smashed on the floor, and her filing cabinet looked like it had been kicked in and emptied. The drawers in her desk were also emptied and tossed on the floor. It looked like a small tornado had ripped the room apart.

Diana stood with her back to him, gazing out the window. "I didn't touch anything. Not that it matters, I suppose. The police dusted for prints, but I'm guessing the only ones they'll find are mine, yours, Brett's, and the cleaning service's."

Raphael crossed the room and put his hands on her shoulders. "Anything taken?"

Diana let herself lean on Raphael for a moment before straightening her spine and pulling away. "My laptop is missing. Without looking through the papers, I can't say for sure if any are missing, though they would be on the computer network. Without the passwords, it won't be easy to get into them. And the keys to the filing cabinet are missing where I hid them under the potted plant by the window."

Raphael noticed the gobs of dirt strewn about the floor on the other side of her desk. "What time did this happen?"

Diana turned to face him. Her hazel eyes were red-rimmed. "I figure it had to be sometime after six or seven. On Friday, the office is cleared out by six. I called the police a little after eight. It's almost ten now."

Raphael squatted down to right one of the chairs and gestured for Diana to sit. She looked like she might collapse. He gently eased her into it. He then squatted down in front of her. "What were you doing here so late?"

Diana dropped her gaze to her hands. "I knew you weren't home, so I thought I would come here. I left my laptop here when I went down to the docks to check on the status of the shipment for the Hollis contract. I then had a personal errand to run. I wanted to grab the laptop before heading home for the weekend."

Raphael rose. "We'll let the cleaning service take care of this mess. I'm sure you're right about the police. It's doubtful they'll find anything. But we need to know if anyone tries to access the data on the computer. I've got a guy at Rouillard, Wade, who can set trackers. I'll call him when we get home."

Diana rose on unsteady legs and grabbed her purse. "All right. I wish I knew what they were looking for."

It was a question Raphael would find the answer to. There were contracts, contacts, proprietary information, financials, and any other amount of data on her computer. "I'll also have Wade chat with security. Only employees should have access. If someone stole your computer hoping to gain access to confidential information, he'll find them."

"I just want to get out of here."

Raphael gave strict instructions to the building security guard that no one was to enter the building who wasn't a badged employee until an internal investigation was launched. He also stayed on high alert as they headed to the parking deck. He looked over her car before letting her climb in. "I'll be right behind you."

Raphael kept pace behind Diana the entire way home. The list of suspects who might have broken into Diana's office was many. It could be someone not happy Raphael took over the business. It could be an enemy of her father. It could be a disgruntled worker. But why not also trash his office? Why not Brett's office or the secretary's desk?

Raphael locked up the house after them but stopped Diana from going upstairs. "My office."

Diana sighed but complied. Now that they were safe at home, she felt a little steadier.

Raphael stood in the office doorway while Diana took a seat. "Where is your father, Diana? I'm sick of these games you're playing. He's the number one suspect, as far as I'm concerned. I don't know what you two hope to accomplish by keeping him hidden. And I don't buy for a second that he doesn't know I took over Cabotage. It's the only thing on this earth he cares about. And the fact that I not only took over his company but married his daughter has to have him fuming. He could have paid off any number of employees to trash your office and steal your laptop."

Diana's jaw dropped. "You think Lanford did this? I told you he doesn't know. And he still owns shares in the company and still has access to the building. If he wanted something, he could just get it himself without destroying my office in the process."

Raphael gripped the edge of the doorway. "First thing I did when I took over was to revoke his security access. You don't think I'd let him anywhere near Cabotage, do you? I'm tempted to revoke yours."

Diana rose, furious with his insinuation. "You think I trashed my office?"

Raphael crossed to her and took her by the shoulders. "I think this whole situation is suspect. You show up at my office, begging me to give you time before I take over the company only days before I filed with the SEC. You slapped me when I made my indecent proposal, but then you practically jumped at my marriage proposal a couple of days later. And let's just say marrying me and moving in with me would give you direct access to my home and my office. And in turn, your father. Maybe instead of being furious I married you, he decided letting me have his daughter would give him an edge. He stays hidden while I buy up shares and decides to send me his pretty daughter instead of confronting me head on. He isn't above seducing women for his own purposes. He would believe I would do the same. So I get his daughter, and he gets an insider while he tries to figure out his next move."

Raphael watched as Diana's cheeks heated and she glanced at the painting as if she wanted to smash it over his head. But instead of moving, she stayed still in his grasp. "What move, Raphael? You got what you wanted. There is nothing left to fight for. I told Lanford that often enough, not that he ever has listened to me. He doesn't know you now own his company, and he doesn't know we're married. You're going to have to believe me."

"There is one last thing I don't have. Not completely."

* * *

Diana didn't like the look in his eyes. The blue depths of his eyes bore into hers, right before he captured her lips with his. She pulled away for a moment, but his grip on her shoulders pulled her back to him. She froze in his grasp, trying to ignore the lure of his dark kiss. But her body betrayed her, and she found herself kissing him back, her arms coming around him, trying to bring her body into full contact with his.

Raphael's kiss went from angry to passionate in a

breath. He found the buttons of her blouse and tore them open. Her white lacy bra barely hid her full breasts; her nipples hardened under the thin fabric. He lifted the thin fabric over her breasts to her neck. He took one peak into his mouth and sucked hard.

Diana's hips slammed against his as she struggled to get free of the confines of her blouse and bra. Somehow, she managed to get the blouse off and her bra unhooked. With her hands now free, she tugged his t-shirt from the waistband of his pants. He had a bit of height on her, and she only got it to the top of his chest before he released her, but only long enough for him to help her remove it.

Diana knew they should stop. This had started in anger; his words and actions were designed to hurt her, to force the truth from her. But instead of pulling away as she had the other night, her mouth softened and opened under his, and she could tell all of his anger transformed into passion. He wanted her. Had wanted her before. And Lanford's daughter or not, she knew he had to have her. And she was going to let him. Now.

Diana's breath hissed when his teeth grazed her neck. She felt his hands slide down her bare back to the back of her thighs. She would have shrieked when he picked her up, but she couldn't catch her breath. She felt the cushions of the couch against her back, and all she could do was open her arms to him.

Raphael gazed down at her chest, flushed pink. Her blonde hair had come loose from the twist she'd had it in, and he touched strands of it with one hand, while his other hand went under the skirt she had worn to work and palmed her.

Diana's fingers went to the waistband of his jeans. "Raphael, please."

He released her hair and used both hands to pull down her underwear, pushing the skirt up to her hips so he could see her. He released her long enough to grab the condom he had stashed in his wallet. He then stripped off his jeans and underwear.

Diana watched as he rolled the condom on, the eyes of the snake tattoo on his wrist gazing at her. She unhooked her skirt and pushed it off, not wanting it in the way. She whimpered when his full weight came down on top of her.

Raphael took her mouth again, easing between her thighs. "Diana, I don't know if I can take this slowly."

Diana felt the same. Wordlessly she arched her hips against his.

Taking that as an invitation, he slowly but completely slipped inside her. Her body resisted slightly but then accepted him. Her breath puffed against his neck, and her fingers dug into his back. "Okay?"

Diana closed her eyes and smiled. "Yes."

Raphael saw the satisfied smile on her face, pulled almost completely out, and surged back in. He had meant it when he said he didn't think he could take this slow, and his pace increased as her hips ground against him, her thighs squeezing him. Again and again he thrust, his body focused completely on hers, pleasuring both of them, driving them toward and over the edge.

Diana whimpered again and cried out as her body pulsed around his as Raphael surged into her one last time.

Raphael collapsed against her. She could feel the sweat between their bodies, but he took his time before pulling out of her and resting his head on her breasts.

Diana wriggled a bit, the leather couch sticking to her back, but she was content and didn't want to get up quite yet. A day's worth of Raphael's beard was rough against her breasts, but she didn't mind. She sighed against the blackness of his hair when he kissed the tip of her breast, then arched when he palmed her other breast and rose over her to kiss her mouth. She savored the slowness of this kiss, different from the rough, demanding kisses from before.

She could feel the beginnings of renewed interest in both him and her when her phone rang. She vaguely remembered tossing her purse on his desk when they entered the room, forgotten as their argument ensued.

Raphael reluctantly climbed off her and to his feet. Heedless of his nudity, he went to fetch her purse. "It might be the police."

Knowing he was right but slightly embarrassed now to be naked on his couch as he came back to her, she took the purse from him and dug out her phone. Her heart started to pound as she saw who the call was from. Turning her back to him, she answered. "Hi, Jasmine."

Raphael heard the stress in her voice. Not knowing its cause, he disposed of the condom before pulling on his underwear and jeans.

Diana paused, then choked out. "I understand. I'll be there soon."

Raphael grabbed the rest of their clothes and handed her his t-shirt. Despite her tone, he smiled at her torn blouse as he tossed it aside.

Diana pulled the oversized shirt on, then looked at Raphael. It would have to be now. At this moment, with this man, one she was starting to have real feelings for, Lanford would decide to give up and ruin it. Knowing it was the right thing to do, but not knowing how Raphael would respond, she put her phone back in her purse and took the rest of her clothes from him. She was struggling to find her words when Raphael spoke.

"Who's Jasmine?"

Diana bit her lip but then forced out the truth. "Lanford's nurse. We have to go."

Raphael grabbed her forearm. "We?"

Diana nodded. "We."

Chapter Ten

Diana insisted she drive, and Raphael relented. Some of the anger he'd felt earlier was back, but he was controlling his temper. He could tell she was struggling for control, and he didn't want to do anything to cause her to lose her grasp on it.

For Raphael's part, he had several questions he wanted to hurl at her. First and most important was why she had had sex with him? Second, what was this about Lanford's nurse? And third, where were they going?

From there, he wanted to apologize for the accusations he'd hurled at her. Wanted to apologize for kissing her in anger. He knew he had a temper. He usually was able to keep it under control. It almost seemed destined that it was another Kennedy who made him lose it. The first time was when he'd punched Lanford out. There were days when he relished the memory of his fist slamming into Lanford's face.

But then there was Diana. He hadn't meant to grab her. He hadn't meant to kiss her, practically grinding her lips and teeth against his. He wanted to, but couldn't, see her as a carbon copy of her father. She cared about people, she cared about her family, and for some reason he couldn't fathom, she seemed to care about him. He had done nothing to earn her trust or her caring. But when she'd touched him during the rough kiss, her fingers trailed into his hair and caressed his neck. Her mouth didn't pull away; she didn't try to stop the kiss. Instead, she kissed him back, her tongue tangled with his until his temper drained away and an intense passion took its place.

At that moment, there was only one thing that could have stopped him from making love to Diana, and that was Diana herself. But she hadn't pulled away again, hadn't slapped him or shoved him. She'd moved closer, pressing those slim hips against his, allowing him to rip her blouse from her. Those moments inside her had been like no other encounter before, and he didn't know what to do about it, or her. And right now, on this night when the scent of Diana clung to his skin, he'd give anything he possessed for Lanford to once again disappear.

But Raphael was nothing if not practical. He allowed only one question to pass his lips, and not the one he wanted to ask. "Where are we going?"

It was well after midnight now, but she seemed to have no trouble navigating the empty streets. Diana hit the turn signal and took the off-ramp that led to her condo. "We're going to my condo. Lanford is there."

Raphael wasn't sure if it was shock he felt or betrayal. "He's been at your condo this whole time?"

Diana had purposefully waited to answer him until she was pulling into the parking lot. She parked in her space, not too far from the entrance. "Not the whole time. Just wait until you see him. And then you can say, do, or ask what you want."

Raphael slammed the door of her car, and he followed her inside. He stayed quiet in the elevator, keeping his distance from her.

* * *

She feared Raphael's response to what he was about to see. Her brothers had been angry at first, but then their anger had faded to a cross between sadness and confusion. Her brothers didn't need to see Lanford take his last breath. And neither did Larissa. But she had told Jasmine to call her when Lanford's time was near, knowing she couldn't leave him with a stranger in his last moments.

Diana unlocked her condo, not surprised that the living room lights were on. "Hi, Jasmine."

The young woman looked at the tall, dark man standing beside her employer, and her eyes widened. She then stammered her words. "You said to call you. I'd say a few hours at most."

Diana had been told that the deterioration might happen fast. Since his last stroke, he had not woken. She had stopped by earlier in the day, and the sounds he had made were mumblings, not words. He had been restless for a time, but the medication the nurse had given him had calmed him. She had left then, knowing that for all intents and purposes, her father was gone.

Diana set her purse down. "You can go. I'll stay. I'll call the agency when it's over."

Jasmine didn't need further urging. She grabbed her bag and was out of the apartment with barely a word.

Diana took Raphael's hand and was grateful when he didn't pull away. She led him to what had once been her bedroom.

Raphael's swift intake of breath was the only sound he made. He glanced at Diana, who was simply staring at her father. He put an arm around her shoulders and walked them toward the bed.

The man in the hospital bed was a shell of the person he'd once been. Once an active and vibrant man, though a cruel and uncaring one, he looked half his size under the white sheet and blanket that covered him. There were no monitors, no mechanical signs of life. The rise of his chest was the only sign he was alive, and even that was few and far between.

Raphael dropped his arm. "This is what you've been hiding."

Diana pulled up a kitchen chair she'd set in the room. She sat beside her father. "Up until a few days ago, he was awake and aware. Or mostly. We fought the day I first came to your office. He wanted to fight you. I told him there was nothing left to fight for. That he'd lost. He was furious with me, of course, for going to you. But the tumor in his brain made him forget we'd even had the conversation. He's spent his last few weeks alone, other than Jasmine, a second nurse who covers Jasmine's days off, and me. I didn't want anyone to know. I needed more time. If word had gotten out that Lanford was dying, the company's shares would have tanked. The company might be publicly held, but Lanford controlled everything about the company, and the board was content to let him since he got results. I needed time to finish securing the contracts and bolstering the board's confidence in me, to keep the company afloat upon Lanford's death."

Now he knew why she wanted three months and how she planned to get control of Lanford's shares. "How long has he been sick?"

Diana leaned back in the chair, her eyes on her father. "He was still working after he was diagnosed with the tumor. The doctors wanted to do surgery, and at that point, Lanford thought he could beat it. The day before his surgery was his last day in the office. I promised him I would take control until he was back on his feet. Then he had a stroke and any chance of him getting back on his feet dimmed. The cancer spread quickly after that, and the doctor stopped chemotherapy and radiation. He gave Lanford three to six months. I gave him three tops when I came to see you. You'd been buying up shares. I knew it was you. Lanford knew one day he'd have to fight you off. I guess neither of us thought he'd do it from a hospital bed. And neither of us thought I'd have to be the one to surrender to you on his behalf."

Diana didn't wait for him to respond. "You don't have to stay, Raphael. This could take a while. And when it's done, I'll get out of your life."

Raphael heard the words but brushed them off. "You owe me six months. You will give it to me. And then I'll give you the money for those shares as I promised. I guess you were right. But why you? Why not your brothers or Larissa?"

Diana yawned, but she didn't think sleep was going to come tonight. "I made Lanford write a will as part of the agreement I'd take over Cabotage. He never thought it would come to this. He was convinced the will was a waste of time; that once he was better, he'd simply have it redone. But I knew. I knew somewhere deep down that this was it. I was granted power of attorney shortly after our marriage. It made dealing with the contracts easier, and the board, though they didn't know, was more than willing to sign control of the company over to you. Your reputation is quite fearsome, as you know. And who better than you to take over when Lanford bailed."

Raphael pulled up the second chair but pulled it to the other side of the bed, away from Diana. "You weren't going to fight me."

Diana glanced at him, the constant ache in her belly worse than she remembered it ever being. She sat up and leaned over, her head between her knees. "No, I wasn't going to fight you. At first, I thought I could stall you. Give people time to react. I thought you were bent on destroying Cabotage. Then you said you would be satisfied taking it from Lanford. But I need the money from those shares for my brothers. If word got out that Lanford was dying, I couldn't take the risk you would change your mind and let the company sink or swim. You are the only person I know who could salvage the business after Lanford's disappearance. I thought that if I could keep his illness a secret and keep the business afloat long enough to secure payment on those shares after his death, then I could reveal his death and let the chips fall where they would. It pained me, though, to know so many people, people who couldn't afford to, would lose their livelihood. When you came to me and made your offer, I didn't have to worry about the people anymore, and I planned to take the money and run once I had them to sell to you. I was going to be safe in New York with friends when news of Lanford's death was made public."

Unable to watch her bent over any longer, to hear her words breaking as she spoke, he went to her and gathered her in his arms. He sighed in relief when she wrapped her arms around his waist and used his strength to keep on her feet. "Come on, there's nothing to be done in here."

Diana let Raphael take her to the living room. He sat her on the couch and gathered her to his side. He grabbed the remote but muted the television when it came on. He flipped to a basketball game and let Diana cry on his shoulder. He could sympathize with her pain, though not with its cause.

Raphael couldn't feel the pity he saw on Diana's face as she spoke about her father. He couldn't feel sorry for Lanford, or even angry. Deep down he supposed he felt relieved. Though Raphael didn't think Lanford would ever try to be a part of Paul's life, a part of him feared it. He feared what Lanford might do in retaliation to an attack on his business. Raphael knew he would do anything to protect his sister and nephew, even if it landed him back in jail. But the only way to stop Lanford was to take away all that he had. It had taken Raphael ten years to get to the point where he could destroy Lanford. And now it seemed he wouldn't truly get the chance. Fate had intervened.

It was maybe an hour later when Raphael eased Diana down on the couch, tucking a throw pillow under her head. He had seen the dark bruising under her eyes and knew she hadn't been sleeping much. He had wondered at its cause but hadn't pushed her. She had told him to accept her secrets or ask her to leave. He wasn't about to let her out of his life, at least not now. And if he were honest, he didn't want her to leave at all. She was soft to his hard. Caring to his dispassionate. And despite her secrets and her outright lies, her heart was in the right place. By taking him up on his offer, she would get the money for her brothers, save the jobs of everyone who worked for Cabotage, and ensure herself a new start when this was over.

He walked to the entryway of Lanford's room. Ben's words came back to him about Lanford's secrets. With Lanford dead, would those secrets go with him to the grave? Diana mentioned a will, but she also had mentioned she'd been through all his papers at his office and his home. She didn't mention finding anything that might be used for blackmail. Glancing back at her sleeping form, he doubted she'd recognize it if she had.

He'd have to see if Diana had Lanford's personal computer. He could have Wade do a deep dive to see if he found any traces of blackmail or a money trail of some kind. Between the man who frightened her outside her office, the crank calls she blocked, and the ransacking of her office, he didn't want to take any chances with Diana's safety.

Dispassionately, he watched as Lanford mumbled a bit and gasped for breath. No doubt, the world would be a better place without Lanford in it. He thought back to Diana's words earlier. What would he have done if he had known Lanford was dying? Diana hadn't known he had no intention of destroying Cabotage when they first met. It would make a nice addition to Rouillard. But seeing Lanford like this, a shell of the man he used to be, he realized Diana was telling the truth. Lanford didn't know he had taken over the company. And he never would.

But Raphael supposed it didn't matter. He would have taken it over anyway. He would have married Diana anyway. His revenge might be a subtle thing, but he'd done what he'd set out to do. And after today, he would never have to worry about Lanford again.

He left the door open and went back to the couch. Taking the opposite side, he grabbed the other throw pillow and laid down. It was a tight fit, but it would have to do. Raphael closed his eyes, confident that Diana would sleep for a while yet. Remembering the feel of her beneath him just hours before, he drifted off to sleep.

* * *

By the time the sun rose, Lanford was gone. Diana had woken with a crick in her neck but was comforted by Raphael's presence on the couch. She slid from the couch, knowing Raphael was now awake as well, and went to her father's room. His body was still under the covers, and she knew he was gone. No tears fell; no grief gripped her. She'd done all the crying she was going to do on Raphael's shoulder last night.

She was grateful when Raphael left to pick up coffee and breakfast. The only caffeine left in her condo was a few cans of caffeinated soda. She couldn't bring herself to open one. She called Larissa and her brothers. She then called the hospice company. The hospice nurse arrived shortly before Raphael returned and confirmed his death. After that, things went pretty fast. The body was picked up by the funeral home she'd selected, and she spoke with them to schedule the funeral service. There would be no open casket and no public viewing. She reluctantly scheduled a wake to give whatever friends or associates Lanford had a chance to pay their respects, not that she expected many. She dreaded the next few days. There was so much to do.

It was almost lunchtime by the time they left her condo. Raphael drove them to a café for a light meal.

Raphael watched as Diana kept stirring the soup she ordered. "Are you okay?"

She stilled. "I guess so. It feels strange knowing he's gone. And yet how many people are better off for it? His life didn't have to end this way."

Raphael thought he understood what she meant. "I always thought him a fool. He had a wife, a daughter, a stepdaughter, and three sons. Other than you, he paid them little to no attention. He didn't realize what a blessing they were. My sister loved him for a time, and he stomped on her heart and tossed her aside. I imagine Larissa loved him once."

Diana felt her eyes sting. "She did. And my mother before her. I loved him once. I can't remember the moment or the day I realized he was not worthy of it. I just remember how I felt. It hurt to know he didn't love me. That he couldn't. And yet I worked for him for years. I always felt, if nothing else, I owed him. Then one day I realized I had more than paid back whatever debt I owed him. That's when I quit Cabotage and took up art full time. Of course, that was also the same time I moved in with Aiden. And then we played at love for a time. Then I realized he didn't love me either, so I left him, too."

"Did you call Ben?"

Diana shook her head. "No. I only told Larissa and the boys. I'll have to make some sort of public announcement. Of course, I had planned to be out of town when I did."

Raphael's eyes narrowed, remembering her comment about New York. "Don't get any ideas. You owe me the six months I asked for."

Diana pushed the soup back, the smell of it making her ill. "As what? Enemies? Business partners? Wife? Lover?"

Raphael took her trembling fingers in his. "How about we start with business partners and lovers? We'll see where we end up."

Diana squeezed his hand. "I'm not sorry about last night."

"Good, neither am I. I'm just sorry about how the night ended."

Diana gazed at their entwined hands. "It's been a long time, Raphael, since I've been involved with anyone. Aiden was the last. I never imagined being involved with you. But despite our argument, you made me feel wanted and desired. It felt nice."

Raphael was taken aback by her candor but gave it back. "You are wanted and desired. And it's been even longer since I've been in a real relationship with a woman. I'm probably pretty rusty."

Diana laughed. "You didn't feel rusty last night."

Raphael pinched her finger. "That's not what I meant."

Diana smiled, feeling content. "I know what you meant. And agreed. Business partners and lovers for now."

"And no New York."

Diana promised. "And no New York."

Chapter Eleven

It was a promise easy to make, Diana mused a few hours later. She had no desire to leave, especially not after what had happened between them. But she also wasn't ready to completely surrender to an affair. When they got back to his house after lunch, she'd been exhausted. She'd left him in the entryway as she headed upstairs to her room. She'd risen a couple of hours later, if not refreshed, at least functioning.

As she lay in bed, the blank canvas in front of her started to call to her. The longer she was under Raphael's roof, the more the urge to pick up her paints grew. She grabbed the sketch pad and pencil she kept tucked in the nightstand and took them downstairs.

"Raphael?" She wandered and realized his office door was closed. She could picture him sprawled out on the couch where he'd made love to her. He had gotten even less sleep than she had.

She took a seat at the dining table where she could see the snake. Its white body was coiled up, and its blue eyes, eyes almost the same shade as Raphael's, gazed at her. She sketched the snake in various poses, the body of each version overlapping the other. She still didn't want to get near it, but she understood Raphael's fondness for the creature. The snake wouldn't demand anything from you. It just was.

She remembered Raphael telling her snakes were a symbol of immortality, as well as rebirth and renewal. Themes everyone at some point in their lives could relate to. But she also remembered reading about the lotus flower, whose various colors meant different things; the pink petals were also about rebirth and regeneration, as well as purity. She sketched a few flowers over the top of the snakes as if they were hiding and revealing themselves within the petals.

How many times had she wished she could be reborn into a new life? How often had she wondered if she would get back some of the innocence she'd had as a young child? They were impossible dreams, and ones she didn't indulge in often. Despite the recent months with her father and her failed relationship with Aiden, she was a contented person. Perhaps she wanted more out of life than she had, but who didn't?

Now she had Raphael. For how long, she didn't know. When he'd taken her in his arms, she'd responded to him with little hesitation. She wasn't one to indulge in affairs, but something about Raphael drew her. Perhaps it was because he'd been with her these last few weeks while her life was spiraling out of her control. Even when they were fighting, she'd found comfort in his presence. She'd leaned on him when she found it hard to stand on her own two feet. She owed him for last night. She hadn't had to deal with Lanford's death on her own. She didn't have to feel guilty anymore for keeping secrets.

Diana glanced at Raphael's closed office door. Well, there was one secret, though a small one. She hadn't told him yet that she was the one who'd painted the seascape on his wall. It was one of a pair of paintings she'd done after she'd left Aiden. She had the other half of the landscape painting in her storage unit. Perhaps that was the way she could repay him for all he'd unknowingly done for her.

She went to the living room and continued her sketching for the next hour, adding dimension and depth to the snakes and flowers.

"I thought you'd sleep longer." Raphael stretched in the doorway of his office, seeing Diana sitting on his sofa with a sketch pad and pencil in her lap.

Diana glanced up; her concentration was broken at the sight of the swath of muscled abdomen exposed as he stretched his arms overhead. She'd touched that skin, had that flesh pressed to her flesh. She felt heat pooling in her belly at the heated memories.

Raphael dropped his arms and headed to grab a beer from the fridge. "Want one?"

Diana nodded.

Raphael popped the tops. He waited until he'd dropped down beside her before handing it to her, his eyes on the pad in her lap. "You've been up a while, I take it."

"I just needed to close my eyes. I hadn't expected to sleep last night. I wouldn't have had I been alone. I owe you for that."

"Not for that." He took a pull of his beer and smiled at Diana when she did the same.

"Okay. Then how about taking over my father's business, but not destroying it? Or how about letting me into your life and letting me meet your sister? Or how about being there when that man confronted me in the parking garage? Or when you came to the office after my office was ransacked?"

He shrugged that off. "I could tell you were getting close to your breaking point. But you wouldn't tell me what was wrong. Being present was about all I could do. But we do need to talk about all of those things. And about last night on my couch, and when that might happen again."

Diana laughed; she couldn't seem to help herself. "Sex was the easy part, I hope. And I don't know when we'll do that again. I just know we will. As for the rest, we should probably talk about that before we explore the personal stuff."

Raphael took the pad from Diana's lap, contemplating it and her. "It can hold for now. I don't know if what happened to your office is about Cabotage or your father."

Diana set her pencil on the coffee table and concentrated on her beer and Raphael. "One and the same, really. I have a lot to do over the next few days. There will be Lanford's service, getting those shares ready to sell to you, putting my condo on the market, and figuring out the best way to tell the public about Lanford's death."

Raphael latched onto the condo comment. "You're selling your condo?"

Diana lifted a brow. "I told you I was moving to New York."

"You said you wouldn't go."

Diana tucked her legs under her. "I said I'd give you your six months. But New York or not, I plan to sell the condo. There is no way I'll live there again. I assume you'll let me stay here."

Raphael set the sketch pad next to her pencil and pulled Diana into his lap. "You'll stay here. Six months or longer. And hopefully in my bed."

Diana scooted until she straddled him. From her position, she could look him in the eyes. "What about your sister? And Paul? We can conduct an affair for a while, but eventually, it will either develop into something more permanent, or it will fizzle out. But what if we get attached and you want me to stay? And if that happens, you can't keep me away from your family forever. You can't pretend I'm not Lanford's daughter, no matter how hard you might try."

"Affair or not, now that Lanford is dead, I won't be able to keep Adeline away. She likes you. And Paul has been asking about you since the wedding."

Diana set her palms on Raphael's chest. "He knows about the marriage, then?"

Raphael brought his hands to her waist, caressing her through her shirt. "He knows. I'll tell Adeline she can set something up."

Shock was a mild word for what Diana was feeling. "I don't know what to say."

His hands slid up her torso, his thumbs brushing the sides of her breasts. "Nothing to say. I wasn't worried about you. Or at least, I'm not worried about you anymore. I was worried about Lanford. But now that he's gone, if Paul wants to meet you and your brothers, I won't stop him."

"Thank you." Diana went to slide off him, but he held her still.

"I want to kiss you first." His lips barely brushed hers, giving her a chance to pull away this time.

Diana leaned into him.

Raphael kissed Diana softly at first, as he should have last night. He cupped her cheeks and took control of the kiss. Unable to resist, he coaxed her to part her lips for him.

Despite a moment of hesitation, Diana let herself enjoy the kiss. He was as masterful at this as he was in everything else in his life. But though the kiss grew heated, she pulled away before it went too far.

Raphael groaned but let her go. When she slid off his lap, he didn't try to stop her.

Diana dropped down beside him and took another swallow of her beer, hoping the coolness of it would help put out the fire in her blood.

Raphael sat forward. He gestured to the sketch pad. "You're good. Will you paint this?"

Diana was a bit bemused by the change in topic but grabbed onto it. "Not my normal style. But it's tempting."

Raphael took her hand and traced the delicate skin of her inner wrist. "You could put a string of those flowers right here."

Diana shivered at his touch. "A symbol of rebirth and renewal to match yours?"

Raphael brought her wrist to his lips, and he kissed her skin, tracing a vein with the tip of his tongue. "Suits you more than my snake. But in a way, with Lanford gone, you're free too."

Diana sighed and let her hand rest in Raphael's. "Almost. I won't be truly free of him until his death is announced, and we figure out who trashed my office and why."

Raphael traced the lines in her palm. "I have some ideas. Do you have your father's work or personal computer?"

Diana pulled her hand to her lap. It was too hard to concentrate when he was touching her. "He had just the one, and yes, I have it. He used his work computer for everything. If there is anything to find, it would be there."

"We'll take it to Rouillard tomorrow. Wade is still trying to see if he can track your stolen laptop. But I want him to take a look at Lanford's computer. The more we know about what he was involved in over the past couple of years, the better I'll feel."

Which brought up another question. "Raphael, why didn't you try to track Lanford down? Medical records are protected, but for someone with the know-how, finding him probably would have been easy."

"I thought about it. Didn't seem worth the effort. Besides, the longer he was gone, the easier he was making it for me to take over."

"Instead, I handed it to you."

Raphael's voice held a tint of anger. "Diana, it's done. He's gone. All we can do is move forward."

The irony wasn't lost on Diana that instead of moving forward, she was further immersing herself in her father's affairs. If she had any sense, she'd pack up and head to New York despite her promise. But common sense seemed to have deserted her the day she'd set foot in Raphael Rouillard's office.

* * *

Diana clutched Lanford's laptop to her chest as she followed Raphael through the offices of Rouillard. Raphael hadn't mentioned it again last night, and he didn't seem interested in seeing what was on it for himself. In a way, that reassured Diana that she was doing the right thing by dragging Raphael further into the mess that her father had left behind.

Last night after their chat on the couch, they ate dinner, and then Diana worked on her sketch while Raphael read. She'd opted to go to bed alone, though she knew one word from her, and Raphael would have carried her off to his bed. So much had happened in the last two days; she needed to step back and make sure she knew what she was doing. Though lying alone in bed last night, she questioned what it was exactly she was stepping back from. They'd already slept together once. It had been amazing. She didn't know what would have happened if she hadn't gotten that phone call from Jasmine, but the night probably would have ended with her in his bed.

But right now she had other things to worry about other than her relationship with Raphael. She'd once again entered the enemy camp. She was wearing her best suit; the dark gray wool of her skirt hit her knees, her heels showed off her legs to their advantage, and the cream blouse under the matching suit jacket had been pressed that morning. But the eyes following her through the office made her feel out of place.

"People are staring. Your employees are going to think you've defected to the other side if I keep showing up here."

Raphael didn't bother to hide his amusement. "They already know I married you. If anything, they're trying to figure out what it is you see in me."

His thick black hair, his sapphire blue eyes, his muscular chest, his chiseled features, Diana mused, take your pick. She could still remember the impact he'd had on her senses the day she confronted him in his office. And that impact had grown, not lessened, the longer she was with him.

"Come on. Wade's office is at the end of the hall. You'll get a reprieve from all the stares."

Diana picked up her pace.

Raphael knocked but didn't wait to open the door. "Found anything?"

Wade held up a finger, typed a few more keys, then looked at his boss. "Nothing super useful. No one has gotten into Ms. Kennedy's laptop. If they do, I'll know. Otherwise, I've been running that search on Lanford that I should have run weeks ago."

Raphael put a hand on Diana's back and ushered her into the room so he could close the door. "What you find stays confidential."

Wade's blonde eyebrow rose. "Isn't everything? I guess I don't need to tell you he died yesterday."

"And that would be what I mean by confidential. Don't bother looking any further into it. Diana has already given me the details. But what I would like to know is who was looking for him, who it was that approached Diana in the parking garage, and who trashed her office."

Diana took the seat Raphael held out for her, the laptop still clutched to her chest. Wade was around the same height as Raphael, but their looks varied from there. Wade had sandy blonde hair and a beard that would make a surfer proud. His loud purple shirt and faded jeans finished off the surfer look.

Diana glanced at Raphael, but then addressed Wade. "Would it help to have access to Cabotage's network?"

"Already in." Wade gestured at Raphael. "Of course, it was a lot easier to gain access with Raphael's access codes. Much faster than hacking it."

Raphael took the seat next to Diana, but his attention was on Wade. "I know you had to have found something."

"Well, Benjamin Houghton has been pretty interested in Lanford's whereabouts. He has some people looking. I've fed them some information, enough to keep them going on the path I laid out, but not enough to know where he is or what he's been doing. Though he hasn't been doing anything but getting ready to meet his maker. You've been busy, Boss. Cabotage's stock has climbed in the past two weeks."

Raphael growled. "I don't need stock prices."

Wade just smiled. "No, I don't guess you do. Anyway, Houghton has been inquiring into some artwork Lanford owned. He's also been inquiring into some contracts and deals that were pending when Lanford went missing. Deals not found in Cabotage's networks."

That wasn't news to Raphael, either. "He was involved in more under-the-table deals than he was aboveboard ones.

Nothing new there. Compile a list of the players. I want to look them over. And Diana, you can look them over as well. You might recognize some of the names."

Diana gaped. "What do you mean by more under-the-table deals than aboveboard?"

Raphael took the laptop from her and handed it to Wade. "According to Ben, your father was involved in some pretty shady dealings. He made claims that Lanford was blackmailing quite a few people."

Diana thought nothing could shock her about her father, but blackmail? Diana leaned over, trying to see what Wade was doing. "Why was Ben looking into the deals?"

Wade kept his eyes on the screen but leaned so she could see better. "Wouldn't hurt to snag some of the business for himself. Depending, of course, on whether they were legal or not. Benjamin Houghton is one tough bastard, but he doesn't do deals under the table or get involved in blackmail, at least not that I can find."

Diana dug her wallet out of her purse. "Here is a sticky note with the username and password. He never changed it. I also added a few others. Faster than hacking, right?"

"I like your lady, Boss. I also have some friends of mine running facial recognition on the guy in the parking garage. Nothing yet. And nothing came up on the fingerprints the cops took from Ms. Kennedy's office. They all match known employee prints. They did find a set that wasn't an employee, but there are no matches on file. So unless they dig up a viable suspect, they won't do much good."

Raphael dismissed that. "It was doubtful they'd find much. They have enough violent crimes to deal with, and a stolen laptop and a trashed office wouldn't make the top of their list. I wouldn't spend a lot of time going over the police reports. I'm looking for anything on that laptop that might be used for blackmail."

"Blackmail, huh? Can do. I'll send you what I find. Guys like Lanford Kennedy like to think of themselves as untouchable. They tend to document things most other people would hide."

Raphael led Diana back to his office. She was a little shell-shocked. This time, as they walked the halls, she wasn't aware of the stares.

Diana sank gratefully into the seat in Raphael's office. She turned her eyes up to his. "Blackmail? How does Ben know that?"

Raphael took the seat across from her instead of behind his desk. "I don't know if it's that big a secret. I knew Lanford was involved in some illegal deals. It was part of the evidence I was gathering to take him down. But I think Ben knows the specifics. He's also worried about those Goodman paintings. We need to go back through your father's papers and see if we can find them. The sooner we unload them on Ben, the happier I'll be."

"But Lanford didn't obtain those paintings illegally. Unethically, to be sure, but it was a legal sale. You can bet Ben would have turned him in for that."

"Would Ben have bought them illegally?"

Diana started to say absolutely not but stopped. She couldn't say for sure he wouldn't have. She turned her worried eyes to Raphael. "Maybe. I think he would have preferred legal means, but he wanted them pretty badly. Do you think he was setting up a deal to illegally buy them when my father offered more for them?"

Raphael took her hand, his touch helping calm her. "I think I should ask him. I didn't think to last time."

Diana wiped the moisture from her eyes with the back of her free hand. "We should ask him then. And we should probably tell him about Lanford."

Raphael nodded. "I think perhaps another dinner on our home turf would be best."

"I'll call him tonight. Right now, I just want to go home."

Raphael dug his keys out of his pocket. "Take the car. I'll catch a ride back tonight. I want to see what Wade finds."

She took them. "Walk me out?"

Raphael followed her to the car. He opened the door but blocked her way. "Be careful. And set the alarm."

Diana was too tired to argue. She went up on her tiptoes and kissed him lightly. "Same goes for you."

Chapter Twelve

Hours later, Raphael closed his front door behind him, exhaustion weighing on him. The living room lights were off, but the light from the kitchen beckoned him. He hoped he and Wade had made some progress, though he wasn't overly optimistic at this point. However, despite the exhaustion, he was still feeling cheerful from when he'd noticed the receptionist gaping at him from behind the glass doors when Diana had kissed him. He knew it would only take an hour before all of Rouillard knew. He had uncharacteristically whistled as he headed back inside and got back to work.

He found Diana sitting at his kitchen table, one of her legs tucked under her, and the other swinging to a silent tune. Her focus was intense as she worked on her sketch. He glanced behind her and saw dinner on the stove. The savory smell drew him to the pot.

Diana glanced up from her sketch, realizing she wasn't alone. "Hi. Dinner is still warm. I made stew."

Raphael grabbed a bowl from the cabinet. "It smells amazing. I'm starving."

Diana set the sketch aside and went to the fridge where she'd left some buttered French bread. She met him at the table and set it down. "Did Wade find anything?"

Raphael took a bite, then another, before answering her. "The better question would be what didn't he find.

Your father had his hand in just about everything, from local business dealings to the art scene, from blackmail to money laundering."

Diana supposed she shouldn't be surprised, but a part of her was. "So it could have been anyone who ransacked my office or who threatened me in the garage?"

Raphael wished he had a different answer, but the truth was best. "Yes. And it could have been two unrelated incidents, which just makes this situation harder."

"What about Chambers? Do you think he might be involved?"

Raphael saw the shudder and the look of distaste on her face. "I don't think so. Ben threatened him, and Chambers agreed to drop his threat to sue you. He's a bastard, but he's a smart one. He knows Ben doesn't make idle threats. And everyone knows Ben adores you."

"I guess I owe him that painting he wants then. I'll have to get it out of storage before he comes over. He'll be here tomorrow night."

"Good. I'm not sure what our move should be as far as a public statement about your father."

Diana nodded. "I bet Ben will have an opinion on that. Maybe he can make the announcement."

Raphael considered it. "It's an idea. We'll see what he thinks. He knows these men better than I do."

Diana bit her lip but asked the question anyway. "I know we talked before, but do you think Ben is involved? I just don't understand why he would have been in contact with these men if their dealings are so shady. I've never known him to cross that line. But though I love Ben, he's not without his faults."

"I don't know. For your sake, I hope not. But I've got Wade digging discreetly into Ben's dealings. We should know more tomorrow."

Diana turned her back and fetched Raphael a beer from the fridge. "I suppose there's nothing else to do but wait."

Raphael gratefully accepted the beer. "You could show me the sketch you're working on."

Diana bit her lip as she handed it over. "I finished the sketch of the snakes and lotus flowers. I'm still debating whether I'll transfer it to a canvas or not. But when I got home and picked up the sketch pad and pencil, only one subject came to mind."

Raphael glanced back at her before turning his gaze back to the sketch. "I think I'm flattered. Do portraits often?"

She'd started with a rough sketch of Raphael's face and shoulders. She'd been adding dimension to his features when he'd come home. In response to his question, she shrugged. "I've been known to. It would be easier, of course, if you sat for it."

"I think I'd rather have you paint the snake."

Diana didn't take offense, but she did take the sketch pad from him. There would always be a part of him hidden away, and the sketch hinted at secrets in his hard gaze. She hadn't softened him up or sketched a more romantic side of him. She wasn't sure he even had one. She liked to think her art was true to life, whether pretty or not. "I take that as a no. I won't paint it if you don't want me to. I've done one of Ben. His oldest son has it. Shandy has one of her and her mother. Nick and Drew never sat still, plus they gave me nothing but grief about a formal portrait, so I did caricatures of them.”

“What about what’s his face? Ben’s son?”

Diana could have sworn she heard jealousy in his voice. But that was absurd. “Aiden. Now that you mention it, no, I didn’t. I suppose that should have been a clue. I’ve painted everyone I love. I even did a rudimentary portrait of my father when I was young. It wasn’t very good, and he was quick to point it out and throw it away.”

Raphael gestured to the sketch pad. “Paint it if you want.”

Surprised, Diana smiled at him. “Will you sit for me?”

Raphael pushed his meal aside and took the sketch pad from her as he rose. He tossed it on the table. “I might be persuaded.”

The sudden heat in his eyes came as no surprise to Diana. She felt an answering heat. She crossed to him and placed her hands on his chest. “What exactly did you have in mind?”

Raphael slipped his hands under the hem of her t-shirt and skimmed the flesh of her back, pulling her flush against him.

Diana’s thighs went lax when he bit her ear and told her in graphic detail what he had in mind.

They were both half unclothed by the time they reached his bedroom. She hadn’t been inside it before, but it wasn’t the décor that held her attention; though peripherally she liked the pale blue and white tones. Their first night together had been rushed, both of them racing to the finish. But tonight she wanted to touch, to see what she hadn't seen the last time.

They both removed the last of their clothing, and Diana gave no resistance when Raphael pulled her down on top of him, and she straddled his waist. She wove her fingers into the dark hair on his chest, loving the warmth and softness of it. She let her fingers linger on his nipples before moving onto the contours of his shoulders and biceps. There was much strength in him, but she didn't feel overwhelmed by that strength. When his calloused fingers caressed her breasts, she arched her back and brought her hands to his wrists.

Raphael sat up and pulled her tighter against him. He reveled in the feel of her breasts pressed against his chest as his hand drifted lower to her core.

She shuddered at the touch of his fingers on her. She used her weight to pull him to his knees and then tugged his shoulders until he was settled between her thighs.

Raphael stopped long enough to dig a condom out of his nightstand. He kissed Diana long and hard before merging their bodies in one powerful thrust.

Diana clung to him as he did the things to her that he had promised in his kitchen and then some. Neither was passive, both clinging to the other until she climaxed beneath him. She was very aware of his release as he practically growled in her ear as he reached it.

Both panting and spent, they lay that way for a time. Eventually, Raphael rolled to the side but pulled her limp body against him. He traced the delicate skin of her wrist where she had laid it over his heart.

Diana opened her eyes and looked up at Raphael through her lashes. "Guess I'll have to paint you now."

Raphael lifted her hand and kissed the skin he'd been tracing. "I think that might be the other way around."

Diana laid her head back down. She knew she would paint him. She'd love to paint him just like this. His dark lashes were lying against his cheek. His muscles weren't tense, and they were still damp with sweat. He looked incredibly satisfied.

She sat up and pulled the sheet up that he'd tossed before they'd fallen into bed. "I suppose this answers my question."

"What question is that?"

"A couple, I suppose. First, I wondered if the other night was a fluke. I feared that maybe I went to bed with you because of all the stress and strain that I'd been under, and you were an anchor in the storm."

Raphael didn't like that question at all, and his face reflected it. "That's crap, and you know it. You were willing to go toe to toe with me to keep me from destroying Cabotage. I've no doubt there are plenty of other men who would have been willing to take you to bed if stress relief was all you were looking for."

Diana sighed but didn't lie back down. "There haven't been any other men for a long time, so one would have been hard to come by. But after Lanford's death, I'm not sure what I was feeling. Tired was the most obvious feeling. So I wondered if we would find ourselves in bed together again, or if once was enough."

Raphael sat up and tipped her chin his way. "Once was

not enough for me. Nor was it for you. You just needed a little time. We still have much to get through in the next few days. And we'll get through them together."

Diana kissed him. "Raphael Rouillard. Who would've thought?"

Raphael kissed her back and pulled her back down to the bed and settled her against his chest once again. "I could say the same. You weren't part of the plan."

With those simple words, she relaxed against him. "So now what?"

"I need to finish dinner."

Diana laughed, and then laughed a little more. "I think I can arrange that, too."

They went downstairs, Raphael finished his dinner, and they went back to bed.

* * *

Diana spent the night in Raphael's bed and had the best night's sleep she'd had in a long time. She knew sex with Raphael complicated their situation, but she couldn't seem to care. They were married, and it had occurred to her that any chance of an annulment was now out of the question, not that Raphael would have permitted one. Divorce was one thing; an annulment was another. But lying next to him, enjoying listening to his breathing as he slept, she knew she couldn't regret the change in their relationship.

She thought back to the sketch. Even in their most intimate moments, and last night there had been many of them, he kept a part of himself held back. She couldn't help wondering if it was her. If she weren't Lanford Kennedy's daughter, would he still hold back? She had a feeling he would. But he loved his sister and his nephew, so she knew he was capable of deep emotions. And it was too soon for her to be thinking about him loving her. But she couldn't help but wonder if Raphael would be able to truly love Lanford's daughter.

But she wasn't able to ponder her deep thoughts for long. Raphael woke, and they made love again before they went their separate ways to get washed up and dressed for the day. She was going to let Raphael deal with Cabotage on his own today, and she was going to go get the painting out of storage for Ben. She'd sent him a text yesterday that she needed to see him, and he was happy enough to come over for another dinner, and she wanted to have it for him. Yes, she was grateful to him for taking care of the problem with Chambers. And though she briefly entertained the idea, she didn't believe Ben was involved in anything illegal. But beyond Chambers, she was going to ask him for an even bigger favor. She wasn't sure she could face the press and announce Lanford's death. She couldn't put it on Larissa. And it didn't feel right having Raphael do it.

Instead of a suit, Diana put on a fresh pair of jeans and a long-sleeved shirt. Raphael kissed her before he left the house, and once he was gone, she grabbed her keys and headed out. The drive to the storage unit helped clear her mind.

Inside the unit were dozens of paintings, some hers, some she or her father had collected. She'd spent hours organizing and cataloging the collection, so she knew where everything was. The first painting she pulled was the winery. Diana set it aside. She had to admit it was some of her better work. She preferred working outdoors. Looking at the lush vineyard, the house in the distance, the sky bright with a few clouds, she could remember the heat on her back, the sun on her face, as she spent hours on the painting. This painting was the first one in a series of paintings that had truly launched her career from hobbyist to artist.

The next one she pulled was the seascape that paired with the one Raphael owned. His was of the day. This one was of the night. She'd spent hours on the section of an isolated beach that had been owned by a friend of a friend. They'd kindly let her roam their property and paint all she wanted. She'd even spent a few nights camping on the rocky shoreline, absorbing the feel of the spray, the smell of the ocean, and the soothing warmth of the wind. She couldn't paint in the dark, but she'd let the memory of the stars overhead and the light reflecting off the water guide her hand.

She wrapped them both in a protective cloth and was getting ready to shut the light off when the portrait caught her eye. It was not one she'd painted. After her father had derided her efforts, he'd hired what he called a true artist to paint him. It had been the last painting she'd unloaded from the truck and into the unit. She'd struggled with what to do with it, but she'd eventually unloaded it. The daughter in her wanted to burn the painting. But the artist in her wouldn't let her.

From an objective standpoint, the painting was quite good. The artist had captured her father's essence. He could be charismatic and charming. He could be cruel and heartless. But at the bottom of his soul, he was just cold. Beneath her father's half-smile, beyond the glint in his eye, the artist had captured the callousness, the disinterest in life that was at the core of who he was. Diana doubted her father saw beyond the surface.

Diana felt a tear fall, and she wiped it away. Part of her wished she could simply forget Lanford ever existed. But then she would not have her brothers. Paul was still beyond her reach, but Drew and Nick weren't, and she wouldn't wish Lanford out of her life if that meant they were gone, too.

Not wanting her father's portrait to be the first painting she saw when she returned, she picked it up and went to put it behind the larger paintings against the far wall. She picked it up from the top, and as she did, she felt something sticky under her fingers. She turned the painting face down on the workbench she had set up when she'd cataloged the art. Tucked against the wood was some putty-like adhesive. Unsure of what it was, she grabbed a tool to pry it away.

Under the adhesive, she found a key inside a small plastic bag as it fell into her hand. She set the tool aside and turned the key into the light so she could see it better. Numbers were etched into the key. It was hard to tell what the key was to. She supposed it could be to just about anything. Diana looked at the stack. Knowing she had no choice, she went over each painting she'd taken from her father's house. After an hour, she had no other keys, papers, or anything else that might explain why her father had stuck a key and a flash drive to the back of his portrait.

Diana tucked the key in her purse, grabbed the two paintings she'd wrapped, and locked the unit. Instead of heading to Cabotage, she headed to Larissa's apartment.

Larissa greeted her warmly and let her inside. "It's good to see you. But I didn't think I'd see you until the service. Drew and Nick are at school."

Diana hugged her purse to her stomach. "I came to see you. I was wondering if I could ask you a few questions?"

Larissa hugged her arms across her chest, mirroring Diana's stance. "About your father?"

Diana nodded.

Larissa sighed and crossed to the sofa and dropped down. "I suppose I should have divorced him years ago. But I can't imagine what you want to ask now that you haven't already asked before."

Diana took a seat in the chair opposite Larissa. "You said you didn't want to fight him, and you wanted your boys to have the best in life. You said staying Lanford's wife was the only way."

Larissa scrubbed her palms over her tired eyes. "I'd say that backfired. Lanford was practically bankrupt before he died. The only thing left was his shares in Cabotage, and even those won't do anything more than pay for Nick's and Drew's school. There is no inheritance for them. And what of Paul? I wanted to give something to him in the event of Lanford's death, but there is nothing for him."

Diana smiled at her stepmother. "I don't think you have to worry about that. I have a feeling Raphael wouldn't let anything bad happen to him. And when it comes time,

I've no doubt his schooling will be paid for, assuming Adeline allows it."

"She seemed nice at the wedding."

Adeline had been reserved but friendly. She and Diana had kept to neutral topics, despite Diana wanting nothing more than to question her about her son. But Diana hadn't pressed, nor would she. In this, Adeline had to come to her.

"Diana?" Larissa leaned forward to touch Diana's hand.

"Sorry. I've not spent much time with her. My marriage is still new, but I have hopes she'll come around."

"And of your father?"

Diana didn't know how to address the subject tactfully. "Has anyone reached out to you about Lanford?"

Larissa stiffened. "A man showed up a couple of months ago looking for him. I told him in no uncertain terms I didn't know where he was, and I didn't care. And as guilty as it makes me feel, I'm glad you were the one who had to deal with him in his last months. And I'm not sorry I wasn't there when he died."

Diana waved that away. "He was my father. And you and I both know the marriage was in name only. You hadn't seen him for months before he took ill. He was my problem, and I handled it. Can you tell me what the man looked like?"

Larissa was confused by the question, but she did her best.

Diana wasn't surprised when her description matched the description of the man who had confronted her about her father at the garage. "Do you know of any safety deposit boxes, storage units, or locker rentals Lanford might have had?"

"If he did, he wouldn't have told me. He was very secretive. I've no doubt there is money hidden somewhere, or a second house, or a safety deposit box of some kind. Your father was always hiding assets. One of our biggest fights was over an account I found that had a couple of million dollars in it but wasn't the one we shared. Our shared account was empty, and I had maxed out most of our credit cards. I was shocked when I found that account."

That sparked Diana's interest. "Do you have any papers or anything to prove it?"

Larissa rose and straightened her trousers. "I hired a private investigator right after I found that account. There wasn't much in the file of any use, but I still have it. I don't know if that will help. And I don't understand why you're asking."

Diana didn't want to burden Larissa any more than she already was. "I'd love the file you have. I know Raphael will want to see it. I can't tell you why I'm asking."

Larissa shuddered. "It's probably best if I don't know anyway. I'm sorry, Diana, but I just want to forget your father. I've done well for myself since I moved out of your father's house. As far as I'm concerned, now that the tuition is settled, I don't care if I ever see another penny of your father's money. I'm leaving the state for good, and I just want to put the past behind me."

Diana glanced at her bag while Larissa left to get the file. If only it were that easy, she mused. If only she could put Lanford behind her and move forward. But until she and Raphael uncovered what her father had been doing all these years, she feared people like the man who confronted her at the garage would keep coming out of the woodwork.

"Here. I don't need it anymore. I hope you have more luck with it than I did."

Diana thanked Larissa, hugged her, and took her leave. Once she was in her car, she opened the folder. Inside it were photos of Lanford with different women. His many girlfriends, no doubt. Diana couldn't help but wonder how much of his money was spent on those women instead of on his children.

There were pictures of him with various men, businessmen from the look of their suits. Ben was featured in a few of them, but that wasn't surprising or incriminating. There were also several other men she recognized from the local business section. She tucked the photos back into the file and flipped through a few more pages.

There were multiple bank statements, tax records, business records, invoices, and copies of deeds and titles to various properties. Diana recognized the bill of sale for the yacht the bank had seized. Beneath those were some typed notes, pages and pages of them. Her eyes crossed as she read the words. Without going through the pages in detail, it was hard to know if there would be anything worthwhile in them. But perhaps the identity of the large man would be in there somewhere.

Feeling exposed, she set the file aside and headed back home to wait for Raphael and prepare dinner for three.

Chapter Thirteen

"You're looking well, Diana." Ben sipped his wine as he contemplated the couple he'd just eaten a delicious meal with. It would have been obvious to anyone that their relationship had moved into the physical. Diana touched Raphael's hand at dinner, and Raphael watched Diana with covetous eyes. The more he got to know Raphael, the more pleased he was with the union.

Diana took her eyes off Raphael's retreating back. He had a call he needed to take, and he closed the door behind him as he went into his office. "What?"

Ben took another sip. "I said you're looking well. You two seem to be getting along."

"We are. Better than I imagined. I can't deny I questioned my sanity a few times. I know you've guessed the real reason behind our marriage."

"Cabotage is not the only source of money and power behind your father. But Raphael taking control of it is a big blow to your father's resources."

Diana didn't mince words. "What do you know about his illegal dealings?"

Ben leaned back in his chair and contemplated his goddaughter. "What do you know of them? Or should I ask, what does Raphael know about them?"

"Raphael has been digging into Lanford's life. Partly because he wanted more ammunition against him. Partly because he wants to know who came looking for me because he was looking for Lanford."

Ben didn't miss the past tense. "Wanted more ammunition?"

Diana folded her hands in her lap. "Lanford is dead."

"What?"

Diana kept her eyes on the table. "He's dead. He was sick. I've been trying for the past few months to keep it hidden. He had cancer. A tumor in his brain ultimately led to a stroke and his death."

Ben contemplated her for a minute. "Because of Nick and Drew."

She nodded. "Yes. I needed the money from the Cabotage shares Lanford still held. And I needed the company on solid footing if I was going to get a decent price. So I came back and took over. Not surprisingly, no one cared where Lanford was, at least at first. It was easy to slip back into a leadership role. Naturally, there was speculation, but most people just didn't care. But then Raphael started buying up shares, and I figured it was all part of a plan to destroy the company. I couldn't let that happen. So I lied to him, you, and everyone else in the hopes of buying a little more time."

"You knew no one would look that hard for him. And Raphael would have assumed the moment he started buying shares, Lanford would emerge from hiding. Except he didn't. Why marriage, Diana?"

"Raphael offered it as a solution. He said it would make the company transition easier. And I think it was another blow to Lanford, marrying his daughter. If things had gone the way Raphael had imagined they would, things would have played out very differently. And we wouldn't have met."

Raphael came back into the room. "Not so differently. You still would have fought for your brothers, even if Lanford had been in the picture. At some point, I'd have found you storming into my office."

Diana glanced over her shoulder to see him smiling at her. "Maybe. And I didn't storm into your office."

Raphael dropped a kiss on her hair and took a seat. "No maybes about it. And you were pretty fierce. You were also quite tempting."

Her eyes spit fire at him. "Are you saying your crude proposal was my fault?"

Mischief danced in his eyes. "I don't recall a crude proposal. But it did cross my mind."

Ben interrupted. "When did Lanford die?"

Diana gave him a brief description of his condition over the past months, her taking power of attorney, and his ultimate death. She left out Raphael's involvement during his death, both before and after.

Ben absorbed what she'd said, and not said. "It's hard to believe the old bastard is dead. And I'm sorry, Diana, but I can't help but be glad he's gone. He hurt a lot of people."

Diana swallowed the lump in her throat. "I don't know what I'm feeling. But I can't say I'm sorry either. In a way, he got an easy out. He never knew Raphael took over the company."

Ben rose and pulled her into his arms. "And you didn't have the heart to tell him."

Diana wrapped her arms around him for a moment. Ben had always been there for her, and she absorbed some of his strength. But she pulled away before she let any more tears fall. "No. I just couldn't. He was dying, whether or not he wanted to admit it."

Ben let her go. "Does Larissa and the boys know?"

"They do. I need another favor from you."

Ben watched as her hand sought out Raphael's. He wasn't surprised when Raphael took it. "What sort of favor?"

Raphael spoke. "We'd like for you to announce his death. I'd like to keep Diana out of the spotlight as much as possible. You and I weren't the only ones looking for Lanford. Diana had a visitor in Cabotage's parking garage a few weeks ago. And then her office was trashed. Someone thinks she knows where he is. I'm not sure if announcing his death will cause his enemies to go back into the shadows or bring more of them out."

Ben understood. "You think distancing Diana from the announcement will hopefully send them back to where they came from. I don't know. As I said, he hurt a lot of people. His list of enemies isn't a short one. And that's why you asked me if I knew about his illegal dealings."

Raphael spoke again. "I know you've been looking into his various dealings. And not all of them are legal that you've looked into. Diana doesn't think you'd be involved in anything illegal. But revenge can be a tricky thing. Maybe you crossed a few lines in the process."

"Because you did?" Ben's tone was firm.

Raphael shook his head. "The only thing I've involved

myself in is Cabotage. I'm a man with a record. I try to stay above board."

Ben relaxed. "All right. I made some inquiries. I even brokered a few real estate deals. But none of them were illegal, though I talked to a few people who think I might be willing to look past a few gray areas to make a few bucks and stick it to Lanford. Announcing his death will probably make those deals dead in the water, so to speak."

Diana just wanted all of this over. "Good. If it forces those deals to fold, all the better. Raphael plans to stabilize Cabotage and then turn it over to his managers. I'll be out of it, and so will Raphael."

"And then what? What are your and Raphael's plans? A blind man could tell you two are sleeping together."

Diana felt her cheeks heat. "We're taking it a day at a time."

Ben turned his eyes to Raphael. "Not good enough. You better make damn sure Diana is safe. You can't be sure Lanford's death will be enough."

Raphael nodded. "Diana isn't going anywhere. She's my wife. And she'll stay that way, at least until she wants to end it. But I won't let her leave until I know this is truly over."

"Good. Why don't you pour me another glass of wine?"

Diana wasn't sure what she should say, if anything, to Raphael's declaration. She opted for silence and left the room while Raphael poured a second glass for all three of them.

She went to the hall closet where she had stashed the key, the file from Larissa, and the two paintings. Not knowing what, if anything, might be useful in the file, she left it on the shelf and brought the two paintings to the kitchen.

Ben sipped his wine. "What do we have here? New work?"

Diana shook her head as she unwrapped the two framed paintings. "You haven't said if you'll announce Lanford's death for me, but I know you will. You've more than earned this."

"The vineyard." Ben set his glass down and lifted the painting Diana had separated from the other.

Raphael didn't look at the painting at first. His eyes were on Diana. There was love in her eyes for Ben, but there was also pride in her eyes as she glanced at the painting Ben had leaned against the table.

"I'm not going to turn this down." Ben kept his eyes on the painting.

Diana turned to Raphael. "I hope you won't turn this down."

Raphael glanced at the painting that was turned away from him. "Did you paint this one, too?"

Diana nodded. The painting in the frame was bulky, but she was used to handling the heavy frames she preferred.

Ben set his painting down and leaned it against the wall. "I don't suppose I need to ask which one you're giving him."

Diana smiled at Ben but then turned serious eyes to Raphael. "This isn't because of what you did to my father. This isn't because you're keeping Cabotage open, or because you're going to pay me for those shares for Nick and Drew."

Raphael crossed his arms over his chest. "No?"

Diana could hear the skepticism in his voice. "Okay, so maybe you have earned this, in a way. I can't say I don't feel guilty for the time you spent in jail. I can't tell you how much I wish I could have affected the outcome of that trial. But I think marrying you and helping you secure Cabotage is enough payment. When we're together, I forget the past. So think of this as a gift for the future."

Raphael accepted the painting from her and helped her turn it so he could see it. She could tell the moment he realized what he was holding. There was no mistaking the curves and smooth lines that matched those of the one hanging in his office. She knew he'd have known it was the same artist even if the subject had been different from the painting hanging in his office.

For a moment, he was speechless. He looked over at the painting he'd barely glanced at when she'd handed it to Ben. "You're D.E."

"Diana Emilia. I dropped the Kennedy. I didn't want any part of my father in my work."

Stunned, his eyes went back to the painting. "It's amazing."

"Thanks."

His eyes went back to hers. "You can't give this to me. It costs a small fortune."

She laughed. "Just the cost of paint and canvas. And if you're worried about it, I can afford to give it to you."

Ben slapped him on the back. "Diana is fabulous and she's getting richer by the day. As long as she gets back to work. So do her a favor and kick her out of Cabotage so she can go back to her paints. She was never able to produce much when she worked for her father. Sucked the inspiration right out of her."

"I can do that." Raphael looked at Diana. "You're fired."

Nothing he could have said to her would have made her feel surer that giving him the painting was the right thing to do. "You can't fire me quite yet. We agreed on six months. But the second the six months are up, I accept."

The rest of the evening was light-hearted. Diana waited until Ben was on the front porch before sharing the time for the funeral.

Ben kissed her cheek. "I'll work with my publicity team, and we'll make the announcement tomorrow morning. Just stay inside until the furor calms. And don't talk to the press. Let Raphael speak for you if you feel you have to say something."

Diana waved him off and went back inside. She found Raphael in his office, the painting leaning against the wall under the one he'd bought.

"I can't believe you're the artist."

Diana came to his side and dropped her head on his shoulder. She sighed when his arm came around her. "Imagine my shock when I saw it on your wall."

Raphael kissed her temple. "I thought you were acting strange. But it was a strange day. In a good way."

"Aiden and I had broken up a few weeks before I painted this. I spent a few days just wandering the shoreline before I began painting. Had I had the money, I'd have bought a parcel of land up there. But I had lost my stock of paintings, so I had a lot of work to do to get enough work together for another showing."

"You lost your paintings?"

Diana realized what she said. She sighed again and leaned further into him. "The art studio where I was having a show burned down. Someone had torched the empty unit next door to the gallery. All of my work, even the ones that had already been sold, were lost. And not just mine. There was another artist whose work was lost. The studio had to refund all the money from the sales. It was quite a blow to my career at the time, and the insurance company didn't pay anywhere near what the paintings were worth. That was the last straw, really. Aiden and I had a big blow-up after the fire. I kicked him out. And then I got back to work."

"If they were on par with these, you must have lost thousands. You're pretty amazing. We'll have to hang these in the living room."

Most walls in his house were empty. She knew exactly where to hang them. "They'll look great on the north wall of the house."

They stood quietly for a time as Raphael held Diana while they looked at the paintings.

* * *

The peace from the night before was short-lived. News of Lanford's death broke early the next morning. Diana's phone rang nonstop. Some of the calls were from people she knew, and she answered those. She accepted their condolences and promised to speak soon. Most calls were from people her father knew, and those she ignored. The local news talked about the recent takeover of Cabotage by Rouillard, and gossip ran rampant about the haste of their marriage.

She'd also turned the file Larissa had given her and the key she'd found to Raphael. He had emailed copies to Wade and a photo of the key. While Raphael spent most of the day on the phone, working from his home office, she had gotten through the first day locked in her bedroom with her paints. She had a small canvas sketched with a pale snake weaving through lotus blossoms. But she had set that aside for a larger canvas. She took Raphael at his word that he would let her paint him. She didn't expect that he would sit for her, but she already knew what she wanted.

But today she had to get through what would hopefully be the last big hurdle: Lanford's funeral. Shandy had flown in last night, and Larissa and the boys had picked her up. Diana had already pulled out a charcoal gray suit jacket and skirt for the service. She opted for black flats. No reason to be uncomfortable all day. She had a feeling it was going to be a long one. The funeral home had promised her that they were used to dealing with the press and wouldn't let in anyone who wasn't there to pay their respects.

"Almost ready?" Raphael stood outside her bedroom door while she finished dressing.

"You don't have to come, you know."

"So you've said."

Diana wasn't sure if his presence was going to make things easier or harder. It wasn't a secret that the two men despised each other. And if anyone had forgotten, various newscasters had reminded the public. When the reminder of Raphael's arrest and incarceration aired, Raphael had had enough and shut the news off.

Diana finished fastening the buckle on her shoe and faced Raphael. "I mean it. You don't have to come."

"You're going to make me mad, Diana. I'm coming. For more reasons than you might think. But let's just say I am not letting you do this alone."

Diana hugged him. "I don't suppose I want to do this alone. But Larissa and the boys will be there."

Raphael gently kissed her. "So will the vultures and the wolves."

Diana kissed him back. "And you prefer snakes."

He brushed the back of his fingers across her cheek. "And flowers. We should go."

Diana trembled under the intensity of his gaze but found herself nodding.

Raphael grabbed her purse for her and the suit jacket she had laid on the bed. "When we get back, we should empty this room. No reason not to keep this as your studio if you like the space, but you don't need the bed."

Startled, Diana stopped fussing with her hair. It was probably silly to play coy now. She'd already spent the past two nights in his room. No reason to think she wouldn't be there tonight, and the next night, and the next. He'd told Ben she could stay until she decided to leave. The longer she was married to Raphael, the less she could picture what her life would be like if she left.

"Diana?"

"Yes. Okay. We can do that."

Raphael took her hand to lead her out. "Good."

Diana ignored the heat in his eyes and followed him out of the room. She couldn't think of a single thing to say on the way to the funeral home.

* * *

Diana was stunned by the number of people in attendance, though Raphael didn't seem fazed. At most, she had expected a couple of associates. Maybe even a mistress. But this mass of people was shocking.

Diana took Raphael's hand as he helped her from the car. She stumbled a bit as they made their way to the entrance.

"Diana!" A pale blonde quickly made her way over.

"Shandy." Diana embraced her stepsister.

Raphael stood back and watched the two women embrace. The younger woman's hair was much lighter than Diana's, her eyes a shimmering blue, and her figure slight. There wasn't much to Diana's stepsister.

"I wish you could have come over last night. But Larissa said you were busy."

Diana gestured to Raphael. "This is my husband, Raphael Rouillard. We were keeping a low profile after Lanford's death hit the news."

Shandy held her hand out to Raphael. "It's nice to meet you. You have Nick and Drew's approval."

Raphael shook the slim hand she offered. "Nice to meet you, too. I wasn't sure when we'd get the chance."

"The wedding took place so quickly, I couldn't get away for it. But I'm glad we could meet, even under the circumstances. I can't believe the cameras and press outside. And who knew Lanford had so many friends?"

The cameras flashed from a distance, and the reporters shouting questions were no surprise to Diana or Raphael. Raphael had used his body to block her from the view of most of the cameras as they made their way inside. "Vultures."

Raphael took a step to be next to Diana's side. "And there are the wolves."

Diana and Shandy turned to see some of her father's associates in a huddle. Diana couldn't hide the disgust in her voice. "No doubt wondering how they can profit from this."

Shandy gave an unladylike snort in agreement. "Several of them called me yesterday. He's not even my father. I hung up on every single one of them."

Raphael approved. "I have the team working on a couple more statements for the press. Our press secretary will deliver them over the next couple of days. Hopefully, they'll slink back to where they came from."

Diana waved at her brothers, who had just noticed them. "The services are private. Family only."

Raphael guided the ladies to their brothers. He greeted them and their mother.

Larissa gave everyone, including Raphael, a quick hug. "I'm glad you're here. I know there's no love lost between you and Lanford, but for Diana's sake, I'm glad you came."

"I wouldn't be anywhere else."

Nick and Drew were quiet. Shandy joined them as they headed to the room that was designated for family.

Larissa's gaze stayed on her children. "Shandy says she doesn't care, but I think some part of her does. Nick and Drew aren't sure what to do or what to feel. I just want this over."

Raphael was going to speak when Adeline came over. "Sorry, I'm late. Paul was excited, and Kevin and I had to convince him to stay home."

Diana turned confused eyes to Adeline. "I wasn't expecting you here."

Adeline glanced around the room. "I'm not here for Lanford. I'm here for Raphael. When he told me he insisted on coming, I insisted as well."

Raphael's voice was a low growl. "I don't need my sister holding my hand. Certainly not today, and not here of all places."

Adeline lifted her chin. "Tough. Let's get this over with."

No doubt Adeline's presence was giving the gossips outside palpitations, Raphael thought. He could imagine the headlines, and it made him shudder. The sooner this was over, the better.

Diana sat in the front with Raphael next to her. Nick sat next to him with Larissa and then Drew. Shandy took the end with Adeline. The two women were whispering. Diana figured they were introducing each other.

Services were short. Raphael knew the only reason Diana had even bothered was for Nick and Drew. He could see tears in the twins' eyes, though none fell. Seeing their confused grief, he knew Diana had done the right thing, even if it did bring out the vultures and the wolves.

Raphael waited patiently by Diana's side as the last of the paperwork was signed; the rest of the people who had come to pay their respects, or to gawk, had left. He held her hand as she thanked the funeral director for taking care of the crowd.

Raphael led the group outside. "Shandy, why don't you ride with us? Larissa, Nick, and Drew, you can ride with Adeline. Larissa, we'll bring you back for your car later."

Diana looked at Raphael. "Did you plan something else?"

Adeline took Diana's hand. "I did. I think it's time Paul meets his family, don't you?"

Diana couldn't respond, only nod. Raphael whispered to his sister before leading Diana and Shandy to his car. "That's why Paul was excited and wanted to come."

When Diana didn't speak, Shandy did. "How much does he know?"

Raphael kept his eyes on the road, glancing at Diana, who seemed almost as if she were in shock. "Probably more than Adeline and I wish he did. Keith is a great influence on him, but he knows Keith is not his real dad. I think a part of him was afraid he'd have to meet Lanford one day. I think he felt a weight lift when he heard his biological father was dead. But he knows he has a half-sister and two half-brothers. I think my marriage to Diana helps him feel less nervous about meeting them."

Diana found her voice. "I wasn't expecting this. Is Adeline sure? I don't want to be responsible for any hurt."

Raphael took her hand. "She's sure. And with Shandy here, it seemed like the right time. Both families get to meet. Ben will be there. Basile and his fiancée will be, too. They just got back. Basile popped the question on the cruise, and she accepted."

Diana felt her lips curl for a moment at Basile's engagement, then nodded and rested against the seat. The last knot in her stomach loosened, and she felt peace for the first time in ages.

* * *

Keith and Adeline's house was packed once the two cars arrived. It was a bit chaotic at first. Paul, despite his excitement, had been reserved. Diana couldn't help but notice the family resemblance between Paul and Raphael. She shook his hand, and they chatted a bit. But as kids do, his reserve drifted away. By the time he'd met everyone, Nick and Drew had convinced Paul to show them his new video game, and they were becoming fast friends.

Adeline came to stand beside Diana. "Okay?"

Diana's voice was clogged with tears. "No. But I will be."

Adeline felt her throat close with the same emotions. "I never thought I'd be able to get Lanford out of his life. I hate that I lived in fear, but I did. I know it's not nice to think ill of the dead or to celebrate their demise, but I'm so relieved."

Diana cleared her throat. "It's okay. I understand, believe me. I'm just so grateful to you for today."

Adeline hugged Diana. "New beginnings."

Diana hugged her back as she looked at the large group. "New beginnings."

"I hear you're a fan of my work." A large man with steel gray hair interrupted the women.

Diana looked up. She smiled for the first time that day. "You must be Basile Rouillard."

"Guilty. I was quite shocked when my nephew told me he'd married Lanford's daughter. I knew his plans, but I didn't recall you being a part of them."

Adeline squeezed her shoulder and left Diana with her uncle.

Diana let Basile lead her to a quiet corner. "I'm not sure Raphael and I would have formally met if I hadn't gone to his office."

Basile laughed. "I hear it was quite the confrontation. But I haven't seen Raph this relaxed in a long time. And I think you're the reason."

Diana searched the room until she saw Raphael. He was standing with Ben behind the three boys as they played their game. "I think our relationship took everyone by surprise. Even us."

"I've met Ben. Raph tells me he's your godfather. Probably a good man to have in your corner. I also hear there has been some trouble."

Diana shuddered. "A man came looking for Lanford. He was getting forceful. Raphael just happened to show up, and the man ran. And someone ransacked my office. They stole my laptop."

Basile nodded. "Wade is on it. If there is anything to

find, or if anyone tries to access the computer, Wade will know. But enough of that. I'm sorry for your loss. Can't say I'm sorry the bastard is dead, though."

"I don't think anyone can be. Sorry, I mean. In the end, he was alone."

Basile looked down at her, his height almost as imposing as Raphael's. "I heard you stayed. It was a nice thing to do."

"Some might say the right thing. I'm just glad it's over. And I'm grateful to the Rouillard family for today."

Basile glanced at his niece. "Adeline is a strong one. Keeps Keith on his toes. But she loves her son more than anything else. She's protected him for eleven years. I'm glad, at least in this, she doesn't have to worry anymore."

Diana could only agree. It was sad how much better off the world was without Lanford Kennedy in it.

The rest of the night, there was nothing but love and laughter. Paul went from slightly reserved to bubbling over with excitement. The adults let the kids get to know one another better while they played games and laughed, and the adults settled in the den.

Diana dropped down on the couch and leaned her head against the back of the couch as she kept her eyes on Adeline and Raphael, who were standing across from her. "I really can't believe you organized this."

Adeline squeezed Raphael's hand before joining Diana. "I'm just glad it's over."

Diana knew she didn't mean the funeral. She remained silent, knowing that nothing she could say would make the past go away.

Kevin sat beside his wife. "Me, too. I don't suppose we truly thought this day would come. But I promised when I proposed I'd never let anyone hurt you again."

Adeline kissed Kevin. "And you kept that promise. Though I knew you would the day I met you."

Diana glanced at Raphael, who was smiling at the exchange. What she wouldn't give to hear those vows come from Raphael's lips.

Chapter Fourteen

As much as Diana would have loved to stay home, she knew she needed to be present at the offices of Cabotage more now than ever. Reporters had been camped outside the offices, and Raphael had promised them a statement later today. She knew he was with the public relations manager going through what he was going to say. Some papers put a positive spin on the story. Raphael Rouillard, the besotted husband, was helping his wife keep her father's company alive while Lanford Kennedy had languished in ill health, despite the past.

Others had dragged Raphael's name through the mud, making her father the victim of what the reporter had coined Rouillard's rage. The biased reporter had made it sound as if Raphael had made Lanford ill and taken advantage of the man's daughter. Diana wasn't thrilled that her name was being tossed around as some hapless damsel in distress. She couldn't help but want to go to the idiot reporter and shove the company's balance sheet in the reporter's face. Diana had been running the company for months, and she knew she'd done a good job of it, too.

Wade had been in touch and was still going through the files. Wade decided it was best to run background checks on several names found within those files, and so far, a few names stood out. He was putting the information together so Diana could go through their pictures and see if any of the men looked familiar. There still was no luck with the key, but Raphael had faith Wade would find what it belonged to.

Diana had been in her office for only half an hour when her door slammed open.

Brett stood in her doorway, his face red in anger. "How could you not tell me?"

Diana was taken aback by his angry tone. "Why don't you close the door, and we'll talk about it."

"You lied to me. You lied to everyone in the company. Do you know what you've done?"

Diana stood. "What have I done, Brett, other than save the company?"

Brett's hands fisted, and he punched his thigh in anger. "You weren't supposed to save it! You were supposed to let Rouillard ruin it. But now the whole world knows you're sleeping with him to save Cabotage. You wrapped him around your little, useless finger, haven't you? I don't know how you managed it. You must be something else in the sack."

Diana felt anger bubble up. "How dare you?"

"I ran circles around your father for years. You weren't supposed to come back. And you certainly weren't supposed to side with your father's enemy."

Diana started to get scared when Brett took a couple of angry steps toward her. "What do you mean?"

Brett was within inches of Diana when the door slammed open. Raphael grabbed Brett by the back of his shirt collar and slammed him against the wall. "Yes, Brett, what do you mean?"

Brett sputtered and took a swing at Raphael.

Raphael kicked his leg from under him and stood over him as Brett fell to the floor. "Are you going to tell her how you've been sabotaging the company for years? Or how you've been putting together illegal deals with Lanford for years? Or how you're the one who trashed her office and stole her computer?"

Ben, Wade, and Basile came into view, blocking the door when Brett would have crawled toward it.

Diana looked at Raphael. "I don't understand."

"Neither did I at first. Brett here has always been the perfect executive. At least on the surface. But he was one of the main contacts for a couple of bad deals your father had put together before he got sick. Ben was contacted by a couple of the people he'd been investigating, and they turned him to Brett. But it didn't stop there. Brett has been playing both sides. He's been selling corporate secrets and working for Cabotage's competitors for years, too."

Brett got to his feet. "You can't prove it."

Wade spoke from the doorway and waved the laptop in his hands. "Raphael might not, but I certainly can. I've got bank records, text messages, emails, phony contracts, and a whole lot more. Some of Cabotage's deals fell through when Lanford disappeared because of you."

Brett spat at Raphael. "And why do you care? You hated Lanford. You swore revenge. When you started buying up shares, I liquidated. But you came and tried to salvage the deals. All over a first-class piece of…"

Raphael closed his hand over his mouth. "Not one more foul word about my wife, or you will regret it."

Brett staggered back. "So what are you going to do? Turn me over to the police? I don't think so."

Raphael took a step forward. "You've been betting on that, haven't you? That I would stay away from the police given my history? Well, you're wrong."

Basile waved to the two men who stood nearby. "He's in there."

Brett was swearing and vowing revenge as he was cuffed and read his rights.

Ben waved Raphael back. "I've got this. I never did like Brett. And when the government is done with him for insider trading, selling government contracts, illegal trading, money laundering, and tax evasion, no doubt Lanford's friends and his enemies will have a field day turning against him to save themselves."

Diana watched Ben leave with the armed men. "I can't believe it. How did you put that together?"

Wade once again held up the laptop. "I'm just that good. I was looking over the names in the file you got from Larissa, and imagine my surprise when Brett's name popped up. Once I started digging, it wasn't hard to track his dealings. I called Ben, and he set up a meeting, recorded the whole shady deal, and then turned it over to the Feds. Turns out they've been watching some of Lanford's friends. Lanford was probably on their list, but that's just my best guess. They weren't exactly forthcoming."

Diana sat down hard. "But how did you put this together so fast?"

Raphael glanced at Wade and Basile. They took the hint and left. "I had my suspicions, Diana. One has to ask himself why a man like Brett kept working for Lanford all these years. Lanford made him a rich man. And Brett didn't seem to have any moral dilemmas playing with and against your father. I talked to Wade the night Ben stopped over, and I had Wade start digging deeper. I called Ben after you went upstairs for a shower. Wade worked all night, and Ben set up the meetings before the funeral. Everything fell into place after that. Basile spent some time helping Wade last night, and I had them come here in case things got ugly. I could hear Brett shouting from my office."

"And you didn't think to tell me?" Diana felt red flags of anger burning her cheeks.

Raphael squatted down in front of her. "Diana, you've had enough to deal with. This was something I could do for you. I'm not going to apologize. I wasn't going to keep it from you after this morning. But Brett moved up the timeline. Wade will get the rest of the evidence to the Feds, and Basile will go back to Rouillard and manage the reports and press for Rouillard. I'll stay here with you, and we'll handle the press on Cabotage's side. And no doubt rumors will be flying at both offices, so we'll need to have a collective meeting with department heads. And no doubt clients on both sides will be calling."

"And?" Diana wasn't ready to let her anger go just yet.

Raphael took her hands in his. "And you needed to get through not only the funeral but meeting Paul. I haven't told you how proud I am of how you and Adeline managed yesterday."

Diana sighed. "You mean because we didn't cry all over Paul and each other?"

Raphael stood and pulled Diana to her feet. "Something like that. Better?"

Diana leaned against him. "Just this once I'll let you get away with it. But no more secrets, not even for a day. Neither of us. Agreed?"

Raphael tipped her face to his. "Agreed."

Diana's lips met his when he bent to her. The kiss was soft and reassuring. When that wasn't enough, she grasped the lapels of his jacket to get closer.

Raphael obliged.

A knock on the door broke them apart. Raphael glanced. "It's Basile."

"Sorry to interrupt. Wade is working with the Feds and Ben is headed back to his office. All hell is going to break loose when the arrest is made public. I hope you're up to the challenge, both of you. Cabotage is about to take a major hit."

Diana nodded. "We've survived worse. And I have faith in Raphael."

Basile smiled. "Don't we all?"

* * *

The phones at Cabotage, Rouillard, and Ben's office blew up exactly four hours after Brett Coleman's arrest. Diana had been more than impressed with how quickly and efficiently Raphael and Basile dealt with the callers and the press that camped themselves outside the office. She didn't get to see Ben in action, but she had no doubt he was handling them with his usual aplomb.

Rumors ran wild at the office, and Raphael quickly and easily soothed the ruffled feathers of Cabotage's staff. It didn't surprise Diana at all that the leaders of the company were already willing to look to Raphael for his leadership and guidance. She might as well not have been in the room. And that was the way she wanted it.

The business reporters had a field day. They had Lanford's death, Brett's arrest, and Raphael's presence at Cabotage as hearty meat for their stories. Raphael ignored the stock prices as they plummeted, knowing they would rise again once the furor died down and people's trust was rebuilt, this time in Rouillard instead of Lanford.

By the time she and Raphael turned off the ten o'clock news, both were exhausted. Raphael's history with Lanford was once again a topic of interest. Their marriage also continued to generate a lot of speculation. Some of which made Diana cringe, and others made her laugh.

"What's so funny?" Raphael clicked off the television.

"The last one was my favorite. As if I'm some sort of femme fatale who has lured you into my web, seducing and tricking you into saving Cabotage from certain doom."

Raphael's brow rose at that. "A bit of an exaggeration, don't you think?"

Diana crawled onto his lap. "You don't want to be lured and seduced into my web?"

Raphael wasn't sure what to make of Diana's mood, but he wasn't going to question it. He lifted her astride his lap and slipped his hands under her blouse until he reached her breasts, pushing her bra up and out of his way. He leaned and kissed her neck, enjoying her shiver immensely. "Think you can lure and seduce me?"

Diana sank further into his lap, rubbing herself intimately against him. "I know I can."

Raphael let Diana take the lead. She unbuttoned his shirt and kissed every inch of his exposed flesh. Her hands found their way into his pants and drove him crazy until he couldn't take it anymore. Getting to his feet with Diana wrapped around him, he carried her upstairs and to his bed.

Diana sighed as he dropped her on the bed and proceeded to strip her. "I thought I was supposed to be seducing you?"

Raphael stripped his clothes off and let her see how she affected him. "Trust me, you have."

Diana wasn't sure who seduced whom, but the fast-paced, passionate lovemaking that followed satisfied and exhausted both of them.

Diana rolled to her stomach after Raphael rolled to his back. She gazed down into his eyes. "I should probably keep this to myself, but I did say no more secrets."

Raphael pulled her on top of him. He kissed her swollen lips. "We did promise."

Diana lifted up so she could see him better. "I love you, Raphael. If I hadn't before, I would have after today. No one has ever tried to protect me before."

Raphael sat up, setting Diana next to him. He looked deeply into her eyes. "Other than Adeline and Paul, I have never wanted to protect anyone before."

Diana hadn't expected him to echo her words, but for a man like Raphael, that was pretty close. But there was one thing she still wanted to know, and perhaps knowing that she loved him, he might find it easier to tell her. She cupped his cheek with her hand. "You don't talk about prison and what happened to you."

Of all the things he might expect a woman to say who had just said she loved him, that was not it. "There isn't anything to tell. Prison is prison."

Diana ignored the hurt she felt when he pulled away from her. She knew it wouldn't be easy for him to talk to her, especially to her, about it. "Raphael, no secrets."

Raphael growled and rolled so that his back was to her. "It's not a secret. Go to sleep, Diana. We have another long day ahead of us tomorrow."

Diana sat quietly in the dark room for a while. Raphael kept his back to her, though she knew he wasn't sleeping. Giving up, she kissed his back. "I do love you, Raphael. I won't ask again."

* * *

Raphael absorbed the feel of her lips on his skin. And he cherished her soft words of love. He hadn't been expecting them from her. Wanted them perhaps, subconsciously. He had already decided he wanted to keep her as his wife. He meant what he said to Ben; she'd have to leave him because he wasn't going to ask her to go. Not ever. Something about her, her presence in his life, filled parts of it he hadn't even known were empty. Perhaps because he was so close to his sister and nephew, he hadn't missed having a woman permanently in his life. But now, with Diana, he couldn't imagine life without her.

Raphael kept his back to her. "It was surreal, at first. I wasn't innocent, to be sure. I had hit the man. But I hadn't beaten him within an inch of his life as he and his attorney claimed. The medical records they produced were manufactured, as was the doctor who testified to the damage I had supposedly inflicted. During the verdict, I was numb. During sentencing, I don't think it had all sunk in yet. I like to think I'm the type who tackles life head-on, not letting myself simply be a participant. But I couldn't seem to grasp the ramifications. But prison cured me the first day. It was all real. It wasn't a bad dream, and it wasn't going away. Your father stole those years from me, but at the time, all I could do was survive each day as it came."

Diana slid an arm over his shoulder so that her hand could rest on his chest.

Raphael closed his eyes and savored her touch. "I'm not going to tell you the details. I had people who you might say were friends. And I had people who were enemies. I defended myself if I had to, and that's all I'll say. Mostly I followed the program. Got myself rehabilitated, whatever that means, and I was released early. It was hard to adjust at first, but I had my family. Though I stayed with Basile, I visited Adeline almost every day for months. I got to know Paul. I hadn't had much money before I went to jail, so by the time I paid off the lawyers, there was no money left. Basile gave me a job, which I was grateful for. I didn't have many job skills after spending my youth on the race track. But I found I was good at the job, and I closed one deal after another until Basile made me stop and take a look at what I was doing to myself. I was slowly working myself to death.

I'm not sure Basile would have noticed if it weren't for Adeline. She does love to interfere."

Diana felt a tear, and she brushed it away before it could touch Raphael's skin. "So what did you do?"

"I built this house. I purposely designed it to be open and airy, unlike the cell I had lived in. I had some vague notion that maybe I would start dating, maybe find a wife, and start a family of my own. I stopped working so hard. I started cooking and going to the gym. I found normalcy and balance."

Diana knew that wasn't all. "And you started plotting your revenge."

Raphael turned so he was facing her. "And I started plotting my revenge. It was just a vague thought during prison. It gained strength as I built my career and reputation. And then one day it solidified as the one last thing I had to do to be truly free."

Diana pressed a light kiss to his lips. "And now you're free. How does it feel?"

Raphael pulled back. "I suppose I am. I'm not sure how I feel about not getting real revenge, but life feels pretty good right now."

Diana smiled at him. "Life feels pretty good to me now, too."

Raphael rolled her onto her back. "You are very lovely, Diana. But you're lovelier on the inside. I'm not sure what fate brought us together, but everything I went through was worth it to be here right now with you."

Diana's eyes teared up. When Raphael lay back down, she laid her head on his chest. "So what about the wife and family part of the plan?"

Raphael tensed. "I have the wife part."

Diana kissed his chest. "So you do."

Raphael relaxed. "Why don't we talk about the family part after this mess is over?"

Diana furrowed her brows. "But Brett was arrested. You said he was the one who ransacked my office."

"But he isn't the one who confronted you in the garage. I still want you to go through those pictures when Wade sends them. We still don't know where that key goes. And we don't know where those Goodman paintings are."

Diana rolled and turned the lamp on. "What do the Goodman paintings have to do with anything? I don't have them."

Raphael bunched the pillow under his head to see her better. "The first night I met Ben, he was concerned about your safety and those paintings. I don't know what the paintings have to do with anything either, but I'd feel better if we knew where they were. If for no other reason than peace of mind. When we find them, you can give them to Ben, and he can worry about it."

"They're valuable, sure, but who else besides Ben would even care?"

"People will do crazy things, Diana, you know that. Maybe the guy in the garage was involved in one of Lanford's shady deals, and that's why the man was looking for him. Maybe Brett knows who he is. But I'll sleep better once all the loose ends are tied. But there isn't anything we can do about it tonight. So why don't you shut that lamp off, curl that sweet body of yours against mine, and go to sleep?"

Knowing he was right, she did as he asked.

Chapter Fifteen

"So how are things going between the two of you, really?" Shandy took a long sip of her iced tea while she and her stepsister watched their twin brothers playing baseball with Paul. Adeline was playing coach and was far enough away that she couldn't hear the conversation between the two women. The three women had agreed to meet when school was out for the day.

Diana rested her chin on her palms. "Not how I expected, I suppose. Though getting to spend this time with Paul has been so nice."

"Paul's great. And he now has two big brothers to look up to. But you know that's not who I meant."

"If you mean Adeline, she's great. I expected to find a very angry, bitter woman, at least where I was concerned. But she's been very accepting of me and my relationship with Raphael. I expected her to hate me simply because I was someone who represented Lanford. She compartmentalizes better than I do. In her shoes, I don't know if I would be as gracious."

Shandy shook her head. "Sure you would. Look how long you put up with Aiden. But I meant Raphael. I didn't get a chance to talk to him much at Adeline's the other day."

The gathering after the funeral had been what all of them had needed. It had truly been a new beginning in some ways. If Lanford had still been alive, Diana wasn't sure if she could have told Raphael that she loved him.

Shandy's voice was soft when she spoke. "Are you okay?"

Diana sat up. She was feeling melancholy today, despite getting another opportunity to be with her stepsister and Paul. She knew it was way too soon for Raphael to have deep feelings for her. The attraction between them was strong, but she wanted more. Unfortunately, she always seemed to want more when it came to her relationships with men. Aiden told her he loved her on occasion, but it was lip service. And Diana had loved him, though that love had slowly died toward the end of their relationship. But she had always wanted more from him, and she wasn't even sure she knew what that something was.

Raphael was very different. He wasn't selfish, he wasn't jealous of her talent, and he wasn't prone to bouts of anger. He had his moods, but in the short time they'd lived together, they weren't really directed at her. At first, he'd been hospitable, making her comfortable. And then they had become lovers before she was even sure of where she wanted their odd relationship to go.

Diana leaned back against the bench. "I'm fine. Just in love."

"Diana! With Raphael?"

Diana found her smile. "Yes, with Raphael. I do try not to be in love with one man while married to another. I'm just feeling a little down today. I told him last night."

Shandy put two and two together. "And he didn't say it back."

Diana sighed. "It's too soon for him. I have a nasty

tendency to wear my heart on my sleeve when it comes to men."

"It's the artist in you. You see deeper into others and into yourself. It's one of the things I've always admired about you and worried about. Most people don't spend too much time on self-reflection. You're always digging out your emotions and using them in your work. It's why you're so good."

"Fat lot of good it does me right now. But I'm telling myself to be patient. We've not been married that long. I just met him last month. But he did open up to me last night. It was more than I expected."

Shandy patted her hand. "Just give him time. Men are slow on the uptake."

Diana raised a brow. "And what do you know of it?"

"Diana, come on. I'm twenty-three. I've had a few boyfriends. What I wouldn't give to have someone like Raphael, though. I do like a tall, dark, and handsome man. And he has a dangerous edge about him. Very sexy."

Diana wasn't about to discuss Raphael with her sister, but she silently agreed. Raphael was not the type of man she saw herself with. Aiden had seemed perfect. They had so much in common, and they didn't have a history between them. But even if Aiden had been the right type of man, Diana wouldn't trade this time with Raphael for anyone else.

Adeline came over and plopped down on the bench. "Man, I'm tired. To have the energy of an eleven-year-old again."

Shandy handed Adeline a bottle of water. "You look

flushed."

Adeline took a long swallow. "Doc warned me I'm not as young as I was when I had Paul."

Diana's jaw dropped. "You're pregnant?"

Adeline took another swallow before answering. "Yes. Kevin and I have been trying for a while. I was starting to get worried I wasn't pregnant yet when I started feeling tired. Kevin is telling Raphael; he probably has by now. We decided it was time to make the official announcement. We told Paul last night. He insisted on seeing Nick and Drew. Said he needed to learn how to be a big brother."

Shandy hugged Adeline and then Diana. "Auntie Diana. How about that?"

Diana looked over at Paul. "I guess I never thought about him being my nephew after I married Raphael."

Adeline gave her a knowing look. "You had a lot on your mind at the time. But if you and Raphael are making a go of this marriage, and it seems like you are, then you're also his aunt by marriage. Believe me, I've thought about it a lot. Which was another reason on my list of reasons, though farther down it, for why I wanted to wait to introduce you to Paul."

Diana nodded, though she wasn't sure she wanted Paul to think of her as an aunt. "Probably pretty far down the list. It's a little awkward. Even stranger if Raphael and I were to have children."

Adeline glanced at Diana. She looked pale. "I didn't realize you two had gotten that serious that you're discussing children."

"Oh, not really. More in the abstract. I had asked him

about his time in jail. And why hadn't he gotten married and had children to fill his home since."

That got Adeline's attention. "He talked to you about his time in jail?"

Diana didn't think she was betraying any confidence, assuming Raphael would have discussed it with his family. "He was a little vague on the details. But I wanted to know. I can see it's had an impact on him, even if he doesn't acknowledge it. He's even agreed to let me paint him."

Diana turned to see tears in Adeline's eyes. "What?"

"If you can get him to talk about it, please keep him talking. He barely said a word for weeks after he was released. He was trying to get back into the routine of normal life. He was trying to get to know Paul as a young child. I can't tell you how many times I cried at the end of the day; he was so closed off. Even when he was back to work full-time and had the house built, he rarely mentioned his time in jail."

Diana felt her throat constrict. Thought about how much trust he put in her that he'd said what little he did say. "I didn't know."

"It was your father who snapped him out of it. I heard about it from Uncle Basile after it happened, but Lanford had gone to Rouillard to confront Raphael. Raphael had snapped up his first of many bids he'd competed with Lanford for. I think Lanford thought he could provoke him. By that time, there was no restraining order or anything. And Raphael hadn't sought him out. Thankfully, Uncle Basile had Lanford tossed out before he could cause any more trouble. Basile wasn't sure what Lanford had said, other than some of the filth he had been spewing when Basile arrived with security. It was that day that Raphael began his campaign to destroy Lanford."

"Did he threaten you or Paul?" Diana felt sick.

"I'm guessing he did, though Uncle Basile was closed-mouthed on the specifics. Raphael barely acknowledged the incident happened. It took him years, but he eventually succeeded in his revenge. I just never imagined him taking Diana Kennedy as a wife. But here we are."

Shandy broke the sudden silence. "Well I, for one, am glad it turned out this way. I'm happy for all of you. Lanford is gone, and you can go on as a family. A real one."

* * *

Diana thought about what Shandy had said about going on as a real family. The seeds were taking root. Diana was happy for Adeline. No doubt this pregnancy would be very different from her first.

But what of her and Raphael? He hadn't told her what he thought of having children with her, other than that they would discuss it later. It sounded as if he was open to the idea. Neither of them was getting younger. Diana supposed they should wait a while, make sure the marriage would last before they took that step. Maybe when this was over, they could go on an extended vacation and spend time, just the two of them, without Lanford or Cabotage between them.

Diana was watching the sunset over the ball field when someone approached from behind. Adeline and Shandy had left to go fetch dinner, and the boys didn't trust Shandy and

Adeline to pick the right food, so Adeline had driven all of them to pick up food to bring back to the park for a final twilight game. Diana had opted to wait and enjoy the quiet.

"You're a hard woman to get alone these days, Ms. Kennedy."

Diana almost fell off the bench; she jumped so hard at the voice behind her. She managed to keep on her feet and spin to face the stranger. The large man behind her was the same man who had tried to confront her at the parking garage. Diana's gaze darted around, but there wasn't anyone nearby. A couple of fields over, some kids were playing, but they weren't going to prove helpful from so far away.

"Now don't get any ideas. I just want to talk. Like I tried to tell you before, I'm a friend of Lanford's. Or I was. I heard he died. It's a shame. It's not right for a man to die before he's had a chance to unburden himself of all his secrets. Or maybe he did. To his loving daughter."

Diana took a few steps back, ready to spin and run at the tiniest provocation. "If you knew my father so well, then you know I'm the last person he would have spilled his secrets to."

The man shifted his weight but didn't come closer. "Brain tumor, wasn't it? Maybe he wasn't in his right mind."

"What do you want from me?"

"I want his secrets."

Not much else of what he could have said would have scared her more. "Any secrets Lanford might have had died with him."

The man did take a step closer this time, his face

coming further into the light from the overhead lamps. "Now why don't I believe you?"

Diana took two steps backward. "You'll have to believe it. I've nothing you want."

"What about good old Ben? I hear he's still looking for the Goodman paintings. Everyone knows you have them."

Not wanting to hear another word, Diana spun and sprinted across the grass. She dared a glance behind her when she reached the parking lot where other people were coming and going. She didn't see him anywhere.

"Diana, what's wrong?" Nick saw his sister as he started climbing out of the car. He could see her skin was flushed, and she was breathing heavily.

"I..." Diana glanced around, but the large man was nowhere to be seen.

Drew came to her side as Nick looked where Diana was looking. "You're trembling."

Diana hugged Drew and took a deep breath. "I'm fine. Someone scared me. But he's gone."

Adeline rolled her window down. "Is something wrong?"

Nick, who heard what his sister said, responded. "Let's go back to Raphael's and eat dinner. He should be home by now."

Paul, who didn't realize something serious was going on, got excited. "I can visit my snake."

Diana looked down. "I left my bag. Give me a second. Drew, why don't you drive my car."

Drew and Nick walked with Diana as she went to retrieve her bag. She saw a note tucked into her wallet. On it was a phone number and a note that said it would be well worth it to turn over the paintings and to call. Though she was tempted to crush it and toss it, she pushed it deep into her bag.

When the whole gang descended on Raphael's house, he appeared taken aback but seemed fine with it. Diana saw his gaze narrow on her and knew it didn't get past his notice that she was pale and trembling.

Not calling attention to it, he bent and kissed her, draping an arm over her shoulder for comfort.

Paul was the first to speak. "We brought dinner, Uncle Raph."

Diana found she could smile at Raphael's indulgent gaze. The smell of pizza was hard to miss, as were the large boxes that Nick and Drew carried.

The noise level grew as Adeline raided Raphael's kitchen. Raphael ignored it. "Are you okay?"

"I'm okay. Just had a fright. That man showed up at the park."

Raphael's fist clenched. "Did he touch you?"

Diana shook her head. "No. We should talk about it after dinner. But you were right. He asked about the Goodman paintings. Well, those and Lanford's secrets. Can we talk about this later?"

Raphael saw Diana's gaze on her brothers. He nodded. "We'll chat later. Let's eat."

Diana relaxed against him.

The adults listened to stories from the afternoon game. Paul was thoroughly enjoying Nick and Drew, and they were being kind and indulgent to their much younger brother.

Adeline handed both of them a plate with a large slice of pizza. "Eat up before the boys do."

Raphael placed a light hand on Adeline's stomach. "Shouldn't you be feeding my future niece or nephew something healthier?"

Adeline placed a hand over her brother's. "No doubt I'll have heartburn later, but trust me when I say he or she wants that pizza."

Diana smiled at Raphael's tender touch and found she had an appetite after all. She left brother and sister, and joined her brothers who had dove wholeheartedly into the box of pizza.

Diana was aware of Raphael's eyes on her most of the evening. He stepped away briefly but wasn't gone long, no doubt to call Wade. By the time the family had taken their leave, it looked like a small tornado had blown through the kitchen. Adeline and Shandy had offered to stay and clean up, but she waved them off.

As soon as Raphael had seen them all safely in their cars, he locked up the house and faced Diana. "Are you sure it was the same man?"

Diana pulled the note from her bag that she'd left on the couch. "I'm sure. When I took off, he slipped this into my wallet."

Raphael held in his anger and took the note. "Probably a burner phone, but I'll have Wade run the number anyway. I called him at dinner, and he should have emailed the file to me by now. Let's go look at the photos he sent."

Three hours later, she had only gotten through half of

them. So far, she had not seen the man who sought her out, and nothing in the bios meant anything to her. Here and there, a business deal or a company name she knew popped up, but since she'd been away from Cabotage, she hadn't been following local business unless, of course, they were interested in buying her art.

Diana rubbed her tired eyes, her blouse long since tugged out of the waistband of her skirt and the buttons around her throat undone. "No wonder it took him so long. Who knew Lanford knew so many people and was involved in so many deals?"

"Not any more than I do. It's part of the job."

Diana continued flipping through and reading the files. Diana gasped as she opened the last file. "It's him."

Raphael stood and placed himself beside her so he could read the screen. "Dwight Finley. Private detective."

Diana glanced over at Raphael. She recognized the name. "He's the private detective Larissa hired. Wade must have run his name because of the files Larissa gave me. Why would he know Lanford? He was spying on him."

Raphael considered that. "It's a good question. But what if, while he was spying on Lanford and digging into his dealings, he decided he wanted a cut of the action? Larissa told you there was nothing in the file of any use. But it was not useful to her as a woman trying to secure a divorce. I read the report he gave her. It read like Lanford was living like a monk, despite the pictures of him with various women. No affairs were mentioned, no shady deals, no partying or drinking. Women always flocked around him, and he made more money on his illegal deals than his legal ones. It's hard to believe that the private investigator wouldn't have found out something worth sharing."

"You think he gave his client a sanitized version. But to what end? Lanford wouldn't have gone into business with a man like Dwight Finley."

Raphael disagreed. "He would if he found him useful. A private detective on retainer, one who was willing to cheat a client, maybe sell secrets, would be exactly the type of man Lanford would have around."

Diana yawned. "So now what? Do we confront him about knowing who he is? Do we turn him over to the cops?"

Raphael leaned over and opened his email. He attached the file and sent it off. "The cops won't do anything. He didn't hurt you; he didn't even threaten you. But maybe Ben knows who this guy is and who else he might be involved with."

"Ok. No cops. But what if Ben doesn't know him?"

Raphael opened an unread email. He smiled. "We go to the storage unit that belongs to that key."

Diana's tired eyes focused on the screen. "Wade found out where the key goes?"

"The storage unit was listed in files Lanford hid on his computer. Wade found bank records for accounts he had drained and some tax forms. It was also full of names, addresses, and phone numbers. The storage place is probably closed, so we'll go first thing in the morning."

Diana wasn't looking forward to it. "Which storage unit?"

Raphael glanced at the file. "Same one where your

paintings are stored."

Raphael shut the computer down and pulled Diana to her feet. He kissed her, lightly at first and then with more passion. "Let's go to bed."

Diana wrapped her arms around his neck and let him lead her upstairs to the bedroom.

Chapter Sixteen

Diana sneezed as she opened the storage locker. "I'm a little frightened to see what he might have deemed important enough to keep in a storage locker."

Raphael sort of understood that. "I doubt he was the sentimental type."

Diana turned the light on. "You'd be right about that."

The storage unit wasn't very full. Padding covered the floors, and wooden pallets held large wooden boxes. Diana's heart started racing. "More paintings."

Raphael tugged the rolling door and closed them in. "We'll need a crowbar."

Diana gestured to a table sitting off to the side. "There's one there."

Raphael grabbed it and opened the first box. "Recognize any of these?"

Diana didn't, though she recognized a couple of the artists' signatures. "I don't remember these. Maybe he had them on his boat and stored them here so they wouldn't get repossessed."

Raphael opened the second one. "These?"

Diana stopped. "That's an Emmet Grayson painting. It's worth a couple hundred thousand. I can't imagine where he got this. Grayson's paintings are extremely hard to come by."

Raphael helped Diana pull the painting out of the crate.

It was abstract with tons of blended colors. "A couple hundred thousand, huh?"

Diana smiled at the skepticism in his voice. "Trust me. The man had a colorful past, almost as colorful as his paintings. For some, the life of the artist makes the paintings more valuable."

Raphael flipped to the next painting.

The one behind the Grayson painting was a pretty boring seascape. Diana recognized the artist. "Aiden Houghton."

Raphael dismissed it. "No wonder you tossed him out. The man has no talent."

It wasn't as bad as all that, but nothing was gripping about it. It didn't tell a story or have any emotions in it. "I wonder why Lanford had this. It has value to a small collector, maybe. But it certainly doesn't belong anywhere near Grayson's paintings."

"Or yours."

Diana took the crowbar from Raphael and opened the third box. Her breath caught as soon as she had the lid off. "What the…?"

Raphael leaned down. The sensual lines and beautiful blending were ones he recognized as hers, even without seeing the signature. "Surprised he has one of yours?"

Diana shook her head. It took a moment to catch her breath. "No, it's not that."

"What?"

Diana turned her confused hazel eyes up to Raphael's blue ones. "This painting was destroyed in the art gallery fire. It shouldn't exist."

Raphael took the crowbar from her limp fingers. There was no soot, no water damage, nothing to indicate it had survived a fire. "You're sure?"

Diana nodded vigorously. "I know every work I've done. I can tell you when I finished it and where I sold it. I keep a photo scrapbook. I'm telling you, this shouldn't exist."

"Then how did your father get it?"

Diana tipped the painting forward to see the next one. She dropped her hand as if the painting were hot. "How?"

Raphael went through the rest in the crate. All four had her signature on them. She nodded to his silent question. "Let's get this in the truck."

Diana took the crowbar back and opened the last crate. "You're not going to believe this."

Her voice was shaking more than it had when she saw her painting. The woman in the painting was quite beautiful. The model had a seductive look on her face, her bare skin glowing gold. Her right breast was exposed from the folds of the sheet that draped over the rest of her torso. It was not Diana's work. The two other paintings in the crate were of the same model in various poses and backgrounds.

Raphael had a feeling he knew who painted these. "Goodman?"

Diana nodded. "Goodman. It's Ben's mother. I need to call him."

Raphael stilled her hand. "Not yet. Not until we know why your father had not only the Goodmans but your paintings as well. I've got a bad feeling."

Diana didn't discount Raphael's instincts. "Okay. Let's get them out of here."

Raphael found a cart, and the two of them managed to get two of the four crates in the bed of the rented truck. The other two they moved to her storage unit, figuring it would be better to have them locked in hers than Lanford's. Right now, he just wanted to get these stashed away.

An hour later, Diana pulled her paintings out of the crate and leaned them against the wall in the living room. "I still can't believe he had these."

Raphael locked his office door where he'd put the crate holding the Goodman paintings, so no one would accidentally see them. "Could they have been delivered to the purchaser before the fire?"

Diana shook her head. "Unless the gallery owner lied to me, all of the work on display was lost. Usually, the gallery displays the paintings until the viewing is over. Any sold ones would then be packed and shipped to the new owner. Any others left over, I would have picked up."

"Did you have any left?"

Diana felt her eyes tear up. "It was a sold-out showing. My career took such a hit after the fire. The police questioned me, as well as the other artist on display. For both of us, our paintings were worth more than the insurance payout. Eventually, the police stopped looking our way. We had nothing to gain by destroying our art. The perpetrator was never caught."

"Maybe whoever started the fire stole them." Raphael pulled her back against his chest, offering her comfort. She'd been visibly upset since she first spied the painting. It was hard to tell which upset her more, hers or the Goodmans, but right now her focus was on her work.

"Maybe. It makes sense. But you'd have to know how to sell them if you were going to make any money. And honestly, I wasn't that well-known back then. It's possible whoever stole them planned to put their signature over mine and sell them as their own. Perhaps the other artist who lost their paintings has some paintings in the crates. I should have checked the signatures. I wasn't thinking."

Raphael wasn't too keen to go back and look, and he said so. "Even if your father had the other artist's paintings, it doesn't explain how he got a hold of them unless he stole them."

Diana wiped a tear. "But that's just it. Why would he? I know he thought I had talent, but you can bet he never told me so. And he wasn't sentimental, so I can't see him buying them from someone else. And I can't see him breaking into the gallery, stealing my art, and burning the place down."

"Maybe our private detective friend knows something about them."

Diana whispered, "It makes no sense. What if there are other paintings out there? I collected insurance money on these. I don't even know where to start making this right."

Raphael kissed her hair. "Even if they weren't burned, they were stolen. You had a right to compensation. Not sure what the process is for recovered merchandise. How many were there?"

"Twenty-four total. Most of them weren't much bigger than these, though there was one large watercolor I did of the Hampton Gardens up north. It was the length of your sofa. You can't just cart that out under your jacket."

"I'll have Wade dig a little deeper into our private investigator. And I'll have him see if he can learn anything more about the fire. In the meantime, you don't go anywhere alone."

Diana simply nodded. She had no desire to be left alone. Seeing those paintings scared her more than she wanted to admit. "What about the Goodmans?"

"We leave them in the crate, locked in my office for now. Ben said having those paintings could put you in danger. I didn't take him very seriously at the time. I was more worried about your father coming out of the woodwork than I was about people looking for three paintings. But perhaps he was right to be concerned."

Diana wasn't so sure. "They're valuable, to be sure. But they're not worth all the hassle. There are other Goodman paintings out there. Ben was the only competition my father had when they were bought behind Ben's back. And when Lanford first disappeared, no one came looking for him, or the Goodman paintings, or anything else. Even Brett wasn't interested in any of that. All he cared about was the company's bottom line. Now we know there was more to it than that, but not once did he mention the paintings, or any deal that might involve them. Ben really should be the only person who cares that much about them."

"And yet a two-bit private eye knows about them and wants them."

"So let me call Ben."

Raphael vetoed that idea. "No. I'm not convinced he's guilt-free in this. I don't like how involved he's been in your father's dealings. He said he was trying to learn more, but what was in it for him? Ben Houghton has always worked above board, or at least that we know of. Why would he warn me to keep you safe and to find those paintings?"

"They're of his mother."

Raphael wasn't buying it. "Sentimentality aside, why else would he want them?"

Diana thought about it for a minute. "To get them from my father? But, Raphael, he's dead. He's no longer in competition with Lanford. No one is. You've got Cabotage, and now I've got the Goodman's. I'd rather get them out of our lives."

"Diana, please. Not until we know more. Why did your father hide them? And more importantly, why did he have your paintings that were supposed to have burned up in a fire?"

"Ok. So now we wait?"

Raphael wrapped her closer to his body. "Now we wait."

* * *

"We need to find answers soon. Your lady is not patient." Wade was furthering his investigation into Dwight Finley. The guy was a certified creep, and there was a lot to sift through.

Raphael, though tired and feeling quite impatient himself, could only agree. "I've sent her out with her brothers. They've decided their wardrobe needs some work. They want to look like college men, whatever that looks like."

"Distraction is good. So far, I can tell you that Dwight is not a well-liked man. Over the last ten years, he's had three restraining orders taken out against him. Seems he likes to smack his girlfriends around. He deposits large amounts of cash, probably from clients who don't want to be tracked. I hacked into his computer. He uses some pretty old software, and he doesn't much believe in digital security."

"Sounds like a peach. Any overlap with Lanford or Ben?"

Wade tapped a few keys. "I can for certain say he knew Lanford. I don't know if you'd call them friends. I retrieved some old text messages between the two of them. They were definitely partners in crime. I found out he knew Lanford when Larissa came to him looking for some dirt against him. The two mocked her in their texts. Dwight promised to put together a nice, useless file for her. After a little more digging, I found that most of the names I put together for Diana were men who refused to do business with Lanford. Sort of an anti-dirt file. Had I not dug into Dwight, we wouldn't be sitting here now."

Raphael knew Wade well enough to know he left no stone unturned. It's why Raphael paid him so well. "I just wish I knew what to do. I'm not going to simply hand those paintings over to Ben like Diana would like me to."

"You think he's involved."

Raphael hated his suspicious nature. He liked Ben but

didn't trust him. "That first meeting between us in private, he was bent on telling me Diana was in danger over those paintings. So far, we have Ben and a private eye looking for them. I don't know what Dwight's intent was when he confronted Diana, but he frightened her. I just can't see how her having those paintings puts her in danger from anyone other than Ben."

Wade interjected. "What about any relatives of Goodman's?"

"The old man died years ago. The daughter owns her own company. She built it up after Ben forcefully took over his grandfather's company. I suppose she may want the paintings because her brother painted them, but from what I gleaned, the son was a mooch, and his death probably was a relief to the family. Wanting the paintings of the woman who bore him an illegitimate child doesn't fly."

Wade digested that. "Probably not. I'll keep digging into our guy. There has to be something we're missing here."

Raphael agreed but just wasn't sure what. "Let me know what you find. I'm going to find Basile."

Wade nodded, his mind already on the task.

Raphael found Basile buried in his screens. "How are things going?"

Basile glanced at his nephew. Raphael had his hands tucked into his pockets, a sure sign he was thinking. "Third quarter earnings report is in. We had a record quarter, but you know that already, even with buying out Cabotage. We haven't talked much about your plans for the company. When you decided to move, you moved fast."

Raphael had purposely waited until Basile was on vacation to make his final move against Lanford. While Basile was on his side, he had wanted to do this on his own. "Cabotage has untapped potential. With Brett out of the picture, we're in a good place to put a permanent manager in place."

Basile's brow rose. "Ahead of schedule. You're that confident?"

Raphael leaned against the doorframe. "I want it done. There are a couple of leaders at Cabotage I think we can promote, and with your help, we can get a new manager trained. By the end of the month, I want to be back here full-time."

Basile leaned back in his seat, mirroring Raphael's pose. "It's not like you to rush things."

Raphael shrugged.

Basile watched as Raphael began pacing the office after shutting the door behind him. "This is about Diana."

"She's given up enough. Did you know she painted the seascape in my office?"

That did get Basile's attention. "You paid a fortune for that painting. It's the first one you bought for your new home, if I recall. She's quite gifted, your wife."

"And that's where she belongs. She doesn't belong in the business world. The faster I can transition Cabotage, the better. She feels responsible for the people there, but beyond that, she'll stay until I leave. So it's time to pass it off."

Basile couldn't fault his logic. "Will she leave you when this is over?"

Raphael could still hear Diana's soft words of love before he told her about his time in jail. "No."

Basile heard something in the inflection of that single word. "And you don't want her to go. I could tell at Adeline's."

Raphael stopped pacing to glance out the window. "I want to build a life with her. A real one."

"I wasn't sure I'd ever see the day. After what happened between you and your fiancée before you were convicted, I wasn't sure you'd give another woman a chance. Prison was hard on you, and you were a changed man when you emerged. I've seen more glimpses of the old you these past few days than I have in years. We have Diana to thank for that."

Raphael rubbed a spot over his heart with the palm of his hand. "I think I'm in love with her."

Basile snorted. "Think?"

Raphael smiled at his reflection in the glass. "I know I am."

"Good. Congratulations. Now go home and tell her. Wade will call if he finds anything, and there isn't anything here I can't handle. Tomorrow we'll start restructuring Cabotage and get both of you out of there."

Raphael glanced at his uncle. "Yes, sir."

* * *

Diana was exhausted by the time she got home. Raphael had texted her earlier in the day that he would be home late. He and Wade were still working on trying to figure out more about Dwight Finley and how some of her paintings had survived a fire. While she wished them luck, after spending the day with Drew, Nick, and Paul, she was ready to put her feet up. Adeline had declined to join them; morning sickness was getting the best of her. So she'd spent the bulk of her day with her brothers. Diana's heart swelled with love for the three young men.

Diana fished her purse and laptop from the back seat and leaned back against the car door after she'd closed it. She glanced up at the house as she did most of the time when she pulled into the driveway. It felt like home, and yet there were still times it didn't seem quite real. There had been so many changes in her life: marriage, her father's passing, meeting her brother for the first time, and making and falling in love with Raphael.

Diana's mind was on Raphael and dinner as she unlocked the front door and disarmed the alarm. She was one button away from resetting the alarm when the door was forcefully opened, knocking her back a couple of steps. She managed to stay on her feet, dropping her purse and laptop as she stumbled.

"Hello, Ms. Kennedy. It's time we finish our little chat."

Diana took a step back as Dwight Finley slammed the door behind him, a large gun in his grip.

Chapter Seventeen

"I want those paintings. I know you have them." Dwight took a menacing step toward her as she backed away from him.

"What are you talking about?"

Dwight grabbed Diana by her shoulder and spun her until she hit the wall. "I saw you and Raphael unload two crates of paintings from storage. I've been following you for days. I knew it was only a matter of time before you figured out where your father stashed them."

Diana winced as his hand tightened on her arm. "Those were my paintings."

Dwight released her and backhanded her.

Diana felt her lip split, and her eyes watered. She found herself looking down the barrel of the large gun.

"You have two choices. You can show me where the Goodman paintings are; I can collect them and leave. Or we can sit and wait until your husband comes home. And when he does, I'll simply shoot him. And by the time I'm finished with you, you'll be begging to give me the paintings."

Diana shivered at the pure evil in his eyes. Raphael wouldn't be home for a couple of hours. Dwight would have them loaded and miles away before Raphael came home. But did she trust him to take the paintings and leave? Did she have a choice?

Diana wiped the blood from her mouth with the back

of her hand. "If I give you what you want, you'll leave?"

"I just want the Goodmans."

Diana glanced at the locked door of Raphael's office. She also gauged her chances of getting past him and out the back door before he caught up to her. She didn't think her chances were good.

Dwight saw where she was looking. "Let's go."

Diana stumbled again when he shoved her toward the office, the gun at her back.

"Open it."

Diana's hand trembled as she turned the knob. She'd known it was locked but doubted he'd believe her.

"Damn. Doesn't even trust you, does he?"

Diana gasped when he pushed her out of the way. Three solid kicks, and he had the door open.

Dwight's eyes were on the crate. "Open it."

Diana wished there were a crowbar nearby, but the crate was only loosely closed. She took the lid off.

Dwight's attention was now solely on the paintings. He was breathing heavily from kicking in the door as he gazed down at the paintings. He lifted the first one out. His eyes ogled the naked breast before he tossed it aside. He then lifted the second one out and tossed it as well.

"And there it is." Dwight lifted the third painting out. The model in this one was wearing a green velvet gown with a beautiful diamond choker and was gazing at the artist with lust in her eyes.

Diana could have wept as Dwight smashed the frame against Raphael's desk, tearing the canvas as he did. While the other two had remained intact after being tossed,

Dwight seemed intent on destroying this one.

Dwight ignored her gasp. He tore the painting from the rest of the frame and then smashed the top of the frame once again against the desk. A small object fell from inside the broken frame. Dwight picked up the object.

Diana saw as he unscrewed a small capsule. A flash drive fell from it.

Dwight held it up to the light. "Do you know what this is?"

Diana refrained from stating the obvious. "I assume it's what you came for."

Dwight fisted the drive. "This is my ticket to the big time. I suppose I should thank you for finding it for me."

Diana didn't like the look on the man's face as he came toward her. She looked around for a weapon, but there wasn't anything within reach. Fear shivered through her as he tucked the drive into his pocket and reached for the button and zipper of his jeans with the hand not holding the gun on her. Revulsion flooded her.

One second Dwight was coming at her, the next Raphael was on top of him. Diana watched in shock as Raphael turned Dwight onto his back and punched the man in the face, then the gut. Raphael managed to wrestle the gun from him, tossing it across the room.

Diana reacted instinctively and went for the gun, but Raphael was on his feet before she could take two steps.

"Are you okay?"

"I'm fine. He has a flash drive in his pocket that he got from the frame of the Goodman painting."

Raphael nodded. "Lanford's insurance. No doubt it

contains the evidence against those he was blackmailing. Our friend here made quite a lot of money working with your father."

Dwight rolled to his knees and then to his feet. He was almost as tall as Raphael, and there was no fear in his eyes as he eyed Raphael. "You'd be surprised by what is on that drive. And I'm not giving it to you."

Raphael wasn't taken by surprise when Dwight lashed out at him, but the man was faster than he looked, and Raphael took a hit to his shoulder. The two men grappled until Dwight was once again knocked to the floor. The man reached into his boot and took out a second gun.

"I learned a lot from the old man. One should always be prepared."

Diana screamed as Dwight turned the gun her way. Raphael lunged in front of her.

Twin gunshots rang through the room, then all was still. Diana clutched Raphael when he fell against her, feeling a wet warmth spreading under her hand. Crying as she held him, she could feel blood seeping into her shirt.

Raphael ignored the searing pain in his shoulder; his eyes were on the doorway as he turned in Diana's arms. "Hello, Ben."

Diana stopped crying long enough to see Dwight on the floor, a bullet in his chest. He looked like he was still breathing. "We need to call 911."

Raphael shook his head and kept his arms around her to prevent her from moving and putting herself in Ben's line of fire. Dwight might not be a danger anymore, but the older man with the gun in the doorway was.

Diana suddenly realized what Raphael had said. "Ben?"

Ben stepped into the room. He glanced at Dwight. "I knew he'd come after you if he knew you had the Goodman paintings. I told you to give them to me. You didn't listen."

Diana tried to step around Raphael again, but his grip on her arm kept her firmly behind him. "I don't understand."

Raphael's voice was firm when he spoke. "Why don't you put the gun down, Ben?"

Ben glanced down at his hand. He had it pointed at Raphael. "I would never hurt her. Never."

Raphael loosened his grip on Diana when Ben dropped the gun in his pocket. "Call 911, Diana."

Both men watched as she dialed and spoke to the dispatcher.

Ben glanced back down at Dwight. "I had to. I couldn't let him hurt her. This is all my fault."

"What is your fault?" Diana slid next to Raphael, her eyes on the blood seeping through his shirt.

"Aiden stole your paintings and burned the art gallery down to cover it up."

"What?" Diana heard the buzzing in her ears as she desperately tried to focus, but it was hard when Raphael was bleeding and seemed unfazed by it.

"Aiden knew you were going to throw him out. Even I had seen the signs. You were good at hiding your feelings, but Aiden was not. Every time I saw you two together, I could feel the anger and distance growing between you. Aiden was so jealous. Jealous of your talent. And he was insanely jealous that you had the career he could only dream of. He came over one night. He'd been drinking. He started talking about what would happen to you if you lost your work. What if it all went up in flames? He said your career would be over. I thought he was just rambling, angry that your relationship was ending. But a week later, I saw the fire on the news, and I knew he had done it."

Raphael knew where this was going. "But you couldn't prove it. So you hired someone who could."

Ben nodded. "I hired a private detective. He found your paintings in Aiden's possession. I was shocked. I assumed he had simply lit them all on fire. But he knew they would be more valuable in the future than they were at that moment. He decided to keep them. I think he thought of selling them as his own, but let's be honest, people would have known they were not his."

"You covered it up." Diana felt the first stirring of anger.

"Not at first. I confronted him and told him he had to turn himself in. He refused. I realized then I couldn't turn him in. I couldn't let my son go to jail. You had insurance, and you started painting up a frenzy. You had another show six months later, and it was a smash."

"So you kept his secret." Diana remembered the dark time after the fire. She fought with Aiden, then threw him out. She had gone up the coast. She'd painted the seascape that eventually hung on Raphael Rouillard's office wall. She still wasn't sure why she kept the night painting that went with the seascape, but something in her hadn't been able to part with it.

Ben looked around the room, his eyes going to the

Goodmans, his eyes tearing up at the torn painting that lay on the floor. He then glanced at the other two. His beautiful mother watched him. "I kept his secret. And I paid Lanford to keep it, too."

Raphael glanced at the man on the floor. "Dwight."

"I had no idea Lanford knew him. Nor did I know that Dwight sold secrets to Lanford. Lanford blackmailed many powerful people, me included. Lanford demanded the paintings. Aiden had managed to sell most of them off for quick cash after he found out I knew what he'd done. I took the four that were left from Aiden and gave them to Lanford. He laughed when I delivered them. Then he demanded money."

Diana couldn't believe the story. "So you just kept paying him?"

"Until he disappeared. I had a few different theories about where he might have gone. One of my favorite theories was that one of his enemies gave him a pair of concrete shoes and dumped him in the ocean. Or he could have blackmailed the wrong person and had to get out of town for a while. A third theory was that he fled the country because the police were after him. I never once imagined he was dying of cancer."

Diana took a throw from a nearby chair and tossed it over the Goodman paintings to stop him from staring at them. "So now what is your plan? Beg me not to turn Aiden in?"

Ben's shoulders dropped. "No. Aiden is currently being held at the police department."

Diana wasn't sure she should believe him. "You turned

him in?"

Ben could barely get the words out. "I did. It was time to come clean."

Diana heard the ambulance getting closer and was grateful as she could see Raphael's pain starting to worsen as he held her. She tried to get him to sit.

Raphael ignored her, his focus still on Ben. "Are you going to tell me why you really wanted those paintings?"

"Hidden inside one of the frames is the evidence Lanford kept. On it are files he kept to blackmail others, and account numbers of all the banks he hid money in. I wanted that file to protect my son."

Raphael growled. "And to blackmail a few people yourself?"

Ben shook his head. "Not blackmail. Leverage, perhaps."

Diana couldn't take it all in. "Dwight knew about the flash drive. When Lanford disappeared, he wanted to find it. And when he died, he really wanted that file."

Raphael bent down and fished the flash drive from Dwight's pocket. He tucked it into Diana's hand. "We'll turn it over to the police. I don't care what's on it."

Diana tucked it into her skirt pocket, then cried out as Raphael collapsed against her. With fresh tears, she helped Raphael sit, and this time he obeyed.

Ben stood still as paramedics came and started working on Dwight. He watched Diana's pale face as a second paramedic worked on Raphael's shoulder. "Those bank accounts should still have money in them. I thought I would take back what I'd paid out. And I knew Raphael would protect you and those paintings when you found them from Dwight. And I thought you would turn them over to me. I'm so sorry, Diana. I never meant for any of this to happen."

Diana didn't get a chance to say anything. The whirlwind of paramedics and police took over. The ride to the hospital was a blur. Raphael's wound wasn't as bad as it had seemed to her, only tearing through the soft flesh of his arm. He grimaced as he got a dozen stitches, a tetanus shot, and a shot for the pain.

She and Raphael gave statements at the hospital, but eventually, they ended up at the police station themselves. She had wanted to wait, but Raphael had wanted it over with. Diana was punchy and tired, but imagining what Raphael was going through as he sat in the police station answering questions kept her from collapsing. How many memories were being stirred up as he sat in a room surrounded by police officers, feeling like he was the one being interrogated? All Diana could think was, thank goodness it was Ben who had shot Dwight and not Raphael. She imagined Ben was in another room answering the same questions and more. But she couldn't find any sympathy for him.

He might not have meant for this to happen, but he'd put her life, and Raphael's, in danger. Had she not found the paintings, what lengths might Dwight have gone to in order to get her to find them? She shuddered thinking about her brothers, or Larissa, or even Shandy, being confronted by him.

As for Dwight, the police had told them he'd made it

through surgery and was expected to recover. He was under arrest and would find himself in a jail cell once released from the hospital.

The detective handling the case came into the room where Diana had been left to wait, with Raphael trailing behind him. She rose and came to him, wrapping her arms around his waist. She let out a small sniffle as he stroked her back.

"Please have a seat." Detective Travis gestured to the empty chairs.

"Can't we go home?" Diana wiped the remnants of her tears from her cheeks.

"I just have a couple more questions. Do you two know what is on the flash drive you turned over?"

Raphael took Diana's hand. "As we understand it, it has what Diana's father, Lanford Kennedy, used to blackmail several different associates of his."

The detective studied the pair, disbelief in his tone. "You didn't read it?"

Diana vigorously shook her head. "We didn't know it was there until Dwight busted the picture frame. And we turned it straight over to the police before we went to the hospital. Even if we wanted to read it, we didn't have time. If you'll recall, my husband was shot."

The detective nodded. "Yes, I recall. There are a few powerful names on this. If any of this turns out to be true, some of these powerful people might find themselves in jail. And the payouts Benjamin Houghton made to keep your father quiet about his son were a significant sum. More money than I'll see in a lifetime. You had no idea?"

"Aiden Houghton stole my artwork, sold it off for pennies, and torched a fellow artist's work. If I had known, I'd have clubbed him and dragged him to the police station myself."

The detective again glanced at the pair, and Diana wriggled in her seat. Diana clutched Raphael's hand as if it were a lifeline. She had no doubt the detective knew of Raphael's past, and she didn't like that he was still questioning their story. But as she looked at Raphael, she couldn't tell if it bothered him to be in an interview room. There was no expression on his face.

"All right. We're done for now. There might be more questions, but right now we're more concerned about Mr. Houghton. His story corroborates yours that he's the one who shot Mr. Finley. And gunshot residue tests for both of you were negative. Your friend might have to test his luck with a jury for his role in covering up his son's crime, but I won't be surprised if tonight's shooting is declared self-defense. His very expensive attorney is already here."

Diana felt a weight lift off her chest. "It was very much self-defense. Or defense of me. I'll testify to that."

Raphael draped his good arm over Diana's shoulder. "We do owe him for that, if nothing else."

Diana relaxed against him. She didn't know if her relationship with Ben would ever be the same, but in the end, he rescued her and Raphael from Dwight.

"You two are free to go. Rest that arm. It's going to hurt like a mother tomorrow."

Raphael tried to ignore the pain in his arm. "It is tomorrow."

Detective Travis nodded at that. And since it was the end of his shift, he offered to drive the couple home. Diana kept her head on Raphael's shoulder and answered a few more questions about her father until the detective finally dropped his questioning.

Diana helped Raphael into the house. She could tell his arm was hurting pretty badly, and he was sagging against her. "Couch or bed?"

Raphael didn't need to think about it twice. "Bed."

* * *

Morning light was streaming through the blinds when Raphael woke. His first thought was that Diana wasn't beside him. His second was that his arm hurt something fierce. He remembered lying down after Diana helped him to bed, but that was it. A combination of pain and drugs had taken over, and he'd thankfully passed out.

Raphael ignored the pain in his arm and went looking for Diana. Sunlight was streaming through the window onto her canvas. She wore a smock over her t-shirt and jeans, her feet bare. Her loose hair fell in waves over her shoulders, and her hazel eyes focused on her work.

He sidled against the wall so he could get a better look from behind her. He saw bright pink lotus flowers on a now-completed canvas set off to the side, a white, blue-eyed snake woven within the blossoms. One had to look hard to see the body of the snake camouflaged in the petals, the blue eyes the only hint of a snake lying in wait.

Diana shifted so Raphael had a better view. She

nodded toward the finished canvas. "I thought it could replace the seascape we hung in the living room. Add some much-needed color to your office."

Raphael came and placed his hands on Diana's shoulders, briefly dropping a kiss on her neck. "I have a feeling you're going to bring a lot of color into my life."

Diana twisted in his arms, looking into Raphael's eyes. His voice had dropped an octave when he'd spoken, and it had made her shiver. "You almost sound like you're looking forward to it."

Raphael pulled her fully against him. "I am. Cabotage will be turned over to a manager this month; I'm transferring the funds for the stock to you today, and you're fired."

Diana cupped his cheeks, kissed him softly, and whispered against his lips, "Raphael, I do love you."

Raphael's lips lingered on hers before reluctantly pulling away. "I love you, Diana."

Shock was a mild word for what she felt at hearing those words. "Raphael?"

He smiled and gave her a fierce kiss. "Surprised me, too."

Diana's smile ended in laughter. "What a mismatched pair we are."

Raphael joined in her laughter. "And yet we fit. But you knew I loved you before I did."

Diana sobered. "How do you mean?"

Raphael turned his eyes back to the canvas she was working on. "It's written all over my face; it's in how you see beyond the surface to the man underneath. It's a dangerous talent, Mrs. Rouillard."

Diana looked at her painting. He was a harsh man; the years had not always been kind to him. But yes, she could see love in him: love for his sister, love for his nephew, and yes, love for her. "I wasn't sure I'd ever have this kind of love. The kind that lasts."

Raphael knew she was thinking of her father, a man who didn't even love himself. And she was thinking of Aiden, a man who only loved himself. Raphael silently vowed to be whatever she needed him to be. And he had no doubt their love would last. When a man waited as long as he had to love and to be loved, he wasn't going to take it for granted.

Diana kissed him again and then stepped out of his arms. "Ready to sit for me?"

"Definitely." With that, Raphael pulled her onto his lap and onto the bed they had yet to clear from the room.

Diana laughed and straddled his hips. She leaned over him as she tugged his shirt over his head. "Perfect."

Epilogue

Diana was helping Adeline as the two women added the final touches to the table of food. Paul was having a blast showing his twin brothers and sister off to his friends. The snake, which Paul named Cupcake, took the place of honor among the table of gifts.

"I can't thank you enough, Diana." Adeline carried in the last platter of food.

Diana took it from her. "It's just a cheese and fruit plate. I think the kids are more excited about the hotdogs and cake."

Adeline bumped her hip against Diana's, as she had seen Diana do when teasing her brothers. "I'm not talking about the food. I'm talking about Raph. I never thought I'd see him so happy. I've seen him smile and laugh more today than I've seen him do in a long time. He loves you and you make him happy."

Diana had to clear her throat before she could speak. "He makes me happy, too."

Diana watched as Raphael glanced their way and whispered something to Paul before heading over. He glanced at Adeline as he took Diana's hand. "You're not carrying anything heavy, are you?"

Adeline placed a hand over her now protruding belly. "Nope. You're as bad as Kevin. I almost feel sorry for you, Diana, when you two get pregnant."

Diana glanced up at Raphael who made her blush with the way he was looking at her. "I don't have to worry about it quite yet, but maybe he'll work it out of his system with you."

Raphael gave Diana a rough kiss. "Don't bet on it, sweetheart."

Adeline's eyes teared up. "Sorry, hormones. I'm so sappy these days."

Diana was about to respond when Kevin came in with Ben at his side. Her fingers squeezed Raphael's hand. They had agreed Paul's birthday party would be a nice, neutral way to see Ben again. Though they had texted, Diana had not spoken to or seen Ben since the shooting.

Ben handed Adeline a card. "Sorry, I bought a gift card. I haven't a clue what twelve-year-old boys are into these days."

Diana's thumb rubbed against Raphael's wedding band. She'd had an artisan friend take her design and make it for him. A coiled snake was etched into the surface. "Snakes."

Ben tried to hide his shudder as he glanced at the large glass tank on the table. "I had baseball cards and a dog. To each his own. Thank you for inviting me."

Raphael smiled as he felt Diana's thumb on his skin. He lifted her hand and kissed the skin over her wedding band. Hers was similar but with lotus flowers etched between the braided edges. "I've got a proposition for you."

Ben glanced at Diana and then back at Raphael. "Not sure I like the sound of that."

"You will."

Raphael led Diana to the outside patio, letting Ben trail

after them.

Ben braced himself, expecting Raphael to deck him, knowing he deserved it and more for what he'd done. But he was surprised when Raphael only spoke.

It hadn't gotten past Raphael's notice that Ben had stiffened, as if waiting for a blow. "I'm going to hit you where it hurts the most. Your wallet."

Ben relaxed. "The Goodman's."

Raphael nodded. "You're going to pay Diana for them. And that money is going to go into Drew's and Nick's college fund."

Diana turned surprised eyes up at Raphael. He was serious. Then she gave him a big grin. "Face value plus twenty percent."

Raphael kissed her upturned mouth. "Twenty-five."

Ben couldn't help his smile at the pair as they kissed, uncaring about who was watching. "Sounds like I'm getting off lightly."

Diana held out a hand to Ben. "Have we a deal?"

Ben glanced at Raphael, then Diana. Ben shook her hand. "Deal. I have something for you."

"What?" Diana reluctantly took the envelope Ben was holding out.

"A list of who Aiden sold your art to. I can't promise the people will be willing to part with your paintings, but they have been contacted by my lawyer that the art was stolen and passed off as Aiden's work. As you can imagine, some of them were quite pleased to learn they owned a painting by the mysterious D.E."

Diana was shocked. "He gave you the names?"

Ben nodded. "It was the least I could do. I demanded and then threatened Aiden until he finally turned over the names."

The statute of limitations was up, so arson and theft charges were not being brought against Aiden. Ben had been visibly relieved, but Diana knew he still felt guilty for his part in the cover-up.

Diana folded the envelope in her hands. "I don't know what to say."

Ben put a hand over hers. "I am so very sorry, Diana. I know none of this has been easy for you, and I know I've damaged our relationship. But I hope that over time you can understand why I did it and forgive me."

Diana wasn't there yet, so she simply nodded.

Raphael wrapped Diana to his side as Ben left the patio. "What are you going to do?"

"Nothing, I suppose. When word gets out, and it will get out, that Aiden fraudulently sold another artist's work as his own, his career is over."

"No loss there." Raphael silently vowed he'd personally make sure word got out if it didn't on its own.

Diana saw the look on his face and was about to speak, knowing exactly what he was thinking, when they were interrupted.

Paul waved at them. "Come on, Uncle Raph and Aunt Di. It's time to eat. Then we're going to cut the cake and open gifts."

Raphael smacked a brief kiss on Diana's mouth which made Paul giggle. "Come on, Aunt Diana, it's time to eat."

Diana let Raphael lead the way.

<u>From The Author</u>

This is my tenth (a milestone!) full length novel. A bulk of it was written during the middle of the pandemic. I'd been sick months before the pandemic started, and the time that followed was not a very productive time for me. So the completion of this novel is quite a milestone for me; the first full-length novel I have published in two years.

Raphael Roulliard is a bit of a throwback character, and I adore him. I will add that I don't like snakes, unless they're behind glass! They are fascinating, though, with all the different colors and sizes they come in. Diana, well, when I first imagined her, I imagined her a little harder, but as I wrote her, I found that while there was strength in her, at her core she was soft.

I hope you enjoyed This Kind of Love! I had a great time Also, if you enjoyed this book, or any of my other titles, please consider leaving a rating at your favorite retailer, Goodreads and/or Bookbub. And if you have the time, a text review would be lovely. Indie authors rely on readers like you to tell others how much you enjoy their books.

Happy reading,

Linny Castle